My True North

Bridget Whitely

authorHOUSE®

AuthorHouse™
1663 Liberty Drive
Bloomington, IN 47403
www.authorhouse.com
Phone: 1-800-839-8640

First published by AuthorHouse 5/21/2009

ISBN: 978-1-4389-8928-0 (e)
ISBN: 978-1-4389-8927-3 (sc)
ISBN: 978-1-4389-8926-6 (hc)

Printed in the United States of America
Bloomington, Indiana

This book is printed on acid-free paper.

In loving memory of Brad Whitely

Prologue

I decided to write this book following the death of my husband. I suppose a part of me wanted every reader to know the injustice one feels when a human life is wrongfully taken. The love we shared was one for which time would stand still. It was a love that created a sense in both of our souls that our commitment was equal and without effort; because of this loss, I find myself dreaming of experiencing love again, yet I feel that to do so, I must let go. Maybe I've already had the only happiness I am entitled to, although I don't believe it. I am re-focusing my attention and healing myself by writing this book which is an effort to begin the process of accepting.

This is our story.

Forward

Ann was raised by a wonderful, strong and resourceful woman. She raised the children on her own with virtually no assistance as her father left their home when the children were quite young. She was close to her sister and two brothers and as they grew up they formed an impenetrable force, sticking together through all of the bad times as well as the good.

By her nineteenth birthday, Ann had fallen deeply in love and had married a man whom she considered to be the most wonderful she could possibly imagine. He had always placed her in the forefront of his mind, and she knew that this man would guide her through life and establish a place in her heart.

At twenty-five years old, Wayne was an exceptional man who would prove to Ann that, she was not only lovable, but capable of returning the love that he gave. When they first met, Wayne immediately felt a connection with her.

By their fifth year of marriage, they had two wonderful boys, Phillip and Andrew. Both were very close to their parents and provided a relationship that most parents only dream of. Life was…perfect.

January 1985

The day when Wayne and Ann first met, they saw an immediate connection instantly. She was sitting at a table on the exterior patio of a local restaurant that she frequented, spending time with a few of her friends when a very attractive man walked past her. He glanced at Ann as he passed by, instantly capturing her attention. The man remained on the patio for a brief moment appearing to be re-considering walking away. He turned back toward her as though he had forgotten something, and walked back to her table, stopped, faced her and bent slightly to speak to her. The smile on his face was one that Ann thought could sink a thousand ships. Instinctively, she knew that this man was not, in anyway, a threat; he had a look that emanated positive feelings. In her line of work, she was very good at "reading" people and reacting on her first impressions. Dealing with the public, Ann had maintained a great deal of self discipline to act first and trust later. In doing so, she had developed a strong talent for self preservation.

"Excuse me, ma'am, I couldn't help but notice you and wanted to introduce myself. My name is Wayne and I am the manager here. Has the service been to your satisfaction?" He held out his hand in introduction. She couldn't help but gently take his hand in greeting.

"Nice to meet you, my name is Ann" she replied with a smile.

"And, yes, everything was fine. I'm just waiting for my friends to finish up, thank you." She gestured to a nearby table where her friends were still picking at their plates of food. She could feel her face turning many different shades of red.

"I was sitting over here just trying to have a bit of quiet time when I saw you. Actually, I'm glad you stopped to talk to me because I was going to ask a few questions."

"Oh?" Wayne asked her with a smile, "Let me see if I can answer them for you."

She was actually at the restaurant with a few acquaintances, but had an underlying motive that they were not made aware of. She was investigating a case of teenage vandalism in the area and was questioning local businesses and homeowners for any clues regarding the suspects.

"Have you seen any teenage kids or young adults in the area that you don't recognize or haven't noticed before? Anyone that looks suspicious to you?" She could tell she was turning red while talking to him. Smiling to herself, she was actually surprised at the attraction she had for him.

"Not that I have noticed, why do you ask? Are you a cop or something?"

"Or something." she replied, again smiling. "I am with the police department and am investigating complaints of vandalism in the area. I have been contacting local businesses and home-owners and thought I would try sitting out here to see if I could find any suspicious activity."

"Any luck with that?" he asked, continuing to smile.

"Not yet", she replied, "but I will give you my card so you can contact me if you see anything."

"Thank you. What if I don't see anything? Can I call you anyway?"

She looked at him, smiling, but didn't say a word.

"Im sorry!" Wayne said. "That sounded terribly rude. Where are my manners?"

"Not at all!" Ann responded quickly. "Yes, I mean, I would like that if you called me anyway...you know, even if you don't see anything... suspicious."

Now Ann was feeling incredibly embarrassed, almost beyond recovery until, smiling, Wayne replied, "Great, cool. I'll do that! Uh, call you, I mean."

He was tall, dark and the most handsome man she had ever laid eyes upon. He looked her straight in the eyes, with a slight twinkle, held out his hand and said once again, "I am very pleased to meet you!" Looking down at the card he held in his hand, he looked up at her. "You are a police officer. Very nice."

"Does that bother you?" Ann asked knowing that being a cop was a turn-off for many men.

"Actually, no. I find it rather exciting that you are one of the individuals protecting me!" Wayne laughed when he said this.

Being a police officer was something that Ann would normally not advertise, but for some reason, she wanted him to know from the very beginning so she could find out whether this would cause him any regret.

That evening, Ann found herself anxiously awaiting the phone to ring. Not surprising, the phone did ring around ten o'clock that evening and when she answered it, she heard an anxious male voice on the other end. They made plans for dinner, but neither were ready to end the conversation. They spent the next few hours getting to know each other having a wonderful time laughing and joking, until well into the next morning.

Wayne confirmed during their first date that Ann was enjoyable to talk to and highly intelligent. He was taken by her wit and found her views and perspectives interesting. They spent a full evening sharing a romantic dinner for two while sipping their glasses of white wine.

Over the next few months, they found themselves wanting to spend time together whenever possible. However, because Ann was working twelve-hour shifts and he was working sixteen, their time was limited and fatigue became a common battle for them both. Her feelings for him were developing quite quickly and had become stronger than she could have imagined. Wayne had a way of making Ann feel young and full of life. Her job was becoming easier to deal with as thoughts of Wayne removed any negative views. However, while she knew that she was teetering on the edge of a deep love for him, he was driving himself so hard with work that the idea of continuing an intimate relationship made Ann selfish.

After several months together, she met him at his work place to discuss their situation. When she arrived, Wayne was busy as usual. As he hadn't noticed her entry yet, Ann was reheared the speech she had prepared for him. She wanted to be sure that if the relationship were to end, she would be able to somehow maintain her composure and they would be able to continue to visit each other, even as friends. She felt very nervous she knew that her reasoning behind this decision was the right one, but not one she was anxious to share. She didn't want to hurt this man, for any reason, nor could she imagine that this decision would not hurt her.

"Well! How are you? I am so glad to see you today!" he said as he approached her with his hands extended as if to embrace her. At this point, feeling remorse for what she was about to do, she asked him if he could step outside for a minute to talk. His face fell. "Of course, can I finish this up first?" he asked.

She waited on the exterior patio for a few minutes. He arrived with a cup of coffee in hand and an extra cup for her. "Please, sit down," Ann instructed.

He took his seat, drew his chair up close to hers, and asked what was on her mind. "Well," she began, "I have been giving us a lot of thought lately. We both are very busy practically working around the clock."

"Ok..."

"Okay, here it goes," she began, "I don't want you to feel that you are under any obligations to me. I guess what I am trying to say is that we should probably end this right here. I'm developing some pretty strong feelings for you and I know that you feel the same for me. I just don't see this working out right now, do you?"

"No," he agreed, "I guess I don't."

"Okay, I suppose that is that. Still friends though, right?" She was upset that he agreed with her so easily but knew that she was making the right decision.

Wayne stood to return to work not understanding completely what had just happened, but knowing that Ann was right. He was developing strong feelings for her as well. In fact, he knew he was falling in love with her. Although he was deeply upset by her decision, he couldn't help but feel a certain sense of relief. Breaking their relationship off at this point left him with the ease of knowing that he would not be pressed to disclose any information regarding his past, information he had shared with no one.

∗∗∗∗∗∗

The following week, Ann learned that Wayne had been fired from his job. She went to the restaurant hoping to see him. Ann was desperate to talk to Wayne. Although Ann and Wayne had "broken up" only a week prior, she still loved him, but she was nervous to see him and knew that she didn't want to end their relationship. Still, she couldn't see how to make this work. She knew Wayne well enough by now to know that he would be able to give her all of him now that he did not have such a demanding job. The problem was, did she?

The following day, Ann received a phone call.

"Hi there." Wayne's voice came across the other end of the line. "I imagine that you heard by now that I was fired last week from the restaurant. The owner accused me of drinking on the job," he said.

"Where is *that* coming from?"

"I don't know," he replied. "He knows I never drink alcohol while working. Heck, I hardly drink alcohol at all. At any rate, he's made his decision, and apparently, he doesn't have to prove it."

"I don't think that really matters now anyway. You should know that I went there yesterday looking for you and one of the employees said the owner fired you for dating the help."

"Oh good!" he said with a hint of sarcasm in his voice. "Now you're stalking me." They both laughed.

Little did they know that this joke would stay with them for years to come. His tone then became serious almost defensive. "You don't believe what you heard, do you?"

"What? That you're dating the help? Please, Wayne! There is no way that I would believe anyone who had anything to say about you. I think we've gotten to know each other well enough to know that we have strong feelings for each other. You would never do that to me or yourself. By the way, please don't think that you *ever* need to justify something so petty to me," she said. "Have you had any luck with the job market?"

"Not yet, it's not so great right now. I really want to get back into welding. With my background, I know that something will pull through real soon for me. Before I worked at the restaurant, I worked as a welding supervisor - building motorcycles, designing frames, things like that. So I've been looking for something along those lines now. Actually, I'm in quite the tight fix, since I didn't see this coming and haven't prepared for it financially. I'm not sure what I will do. My rent is due in a couple of weeks, and so is my truck payment. Things just aren't good right now Ann. I still can't offer you anything more than my heart."

"That's all I want Wayne. I'm on your side, and I'm on my way over. I have something to discuss with you, and I don't want to do this over the phone!"

Ann had been holding on to a ridiculous thought that the two of them could pick up where they left off only days ago. She was hoping that they could begin a life together and be able to provide each other with the support they both needed. She wanted to assure him that his current situation didn't have any impact on the feelings she had and that she would continue to support him, even through hard times. With butterflies of excitement in her stomach, she jumped in her car and headed for his house.

Awaiting her arrival, Wayne realized that he would have to make a decision. If they got back together, he would have to disclose his true identity to her eventually. To do this, he would have to establish a very strong bond of trust with her. No matter how he told her, she would be torn.

✳ ✳ ✳ ✳ ✳ ✳

Opening the door, he smiled. "I am so happy to see you!"

Ann could feel the embarrassment heating up her face. "Always here for a friend. We are still that, aren't we?"

"Well, given my present situation, that's all I can offer right now."

"But...?"

"What do you mean?" he asked.

"You said 'right now'. Do you have something in mind?" She gave him her famous inquisitive raised eyebrow.

"Come on, let's sit down and talk. Do you want something to drink?"

"How about a glass of water?"

Moments later, he joined her in the living room

They sat on the couch, drinks in hand, and she began by telling him how she felt.

"The decision we made the other day was very difficult, Wayne. I never wanted to leave you and certainly don't want to hurt you. I know that in your situation, you're probably not able to make any concrete decisions, so what I really want to do is let you know that your present situation doesn't change the way I feel about you. I love you, Wayne, with or without a job. I love you!"

"I know, sweetie. I love you, too. You're right. I can't make any concrete decisions right now. I'm trying to figure out how I can make ends meet. I do want to stay with you, but I don't know how I'm going to do that right now, until I figure things out for myself. When you left that day, I was heart-broken. I don't ever want to go through that again. I would like you to share your life with me, because, you know something? I love you with all my heart! I realized it for the first time when you drove away and were so angry at me. You stole my heart that first day I saw you, now you've got your teeth in it!"

Ann's heart began to flutter and jump all over her chest. She knew she loved him. Until now, she did not believe that there was any such thing as true love. Now, she knew that she loved this man and never, ever wanted to let go.

"Let's begin a new life together and take things one day at a time!" She held up her glass of water. "Here's to us. Wayne, I want you to know that I love you more than you could possibly imagine!" They gently touched their glasses together in a toast of celebration. Wayne set his glass down, took Ann's from her, and led her into the bedroom.

※※※※※※

During the following months Wayne found his dream job. He became a manager and was very happy with his new life. By the end of their first year together, Wayne proposed to Ann, and she accepted without hesitation. The idea of living the rest of her life with him fulfilled her dreams. Ann would do everything possible for him and he, would move the earth for her. When they married they began a journey together that they both expected would last a lifetime.

By their first anniversary, Wayne and Ann had become known to others as "the inseparable couple." Their friends adored them and others envied them. It didn't take long for everyone to see that they made a fabulous team and had become the best of friends.

In their second year of marriage, Ann became pregnant with their first child. Phillip was born a healthy and strong baby. The three of them became inseparable. The next year brought the birth of their second child, Andrew.

The following year, Wayne had sustained extensive injuries from a car accident. He was on his way to visit with a friend from out of town when he lost control of his vehicle and drove off the road. The impact from running into a guardrail fractured his knee and thigh, requiring extensive surgery. When questioned, he claimed that the accident had been caused when another vehicle had begun to swerve on the highway forcing him off the road. Further investigation demonstrated that the "mistaken swerve" was more intentional than not. It was the investigating officer's impression based on the evidence at the scene and Wayne's vehicle, that he was deliberately forced off the road.

"The damage to the left side of your car indicates that another vehicle hit you more than once. That and the location and type of marks on the pavement. Any idea who might do something like this? Do you have any reason to believe that it may have been intentional?" the investigator asked him.

"I don't know for sure. Maybe this person thought I was someone else." Wayne was trying to make every attempt to let this investigation go. Because of his past and the involvement he shared with certain individuals, he had every reason to believe that there might be someone after him. If there was, he knew it was safer to keep things quiet not only for his own protection, but for his family as well.

The individuals he was thinking of had been left to believe that Wayne was no longer alive, but if they found out differently, well, things could get pretty ugly from here. Better, he thought, to let Ann believe that it was an accident and nothing more.

Wayne had a close friend that worked for the department. He met Chris a few years ago following an altercation at the restaurant. Starting the investigation, and because Wayne was married to Ann, he and Chris had developed a friendship that was kicked off by the interest and concern that Chris had shown initially. He gave the investigation the utmost priority surprising Wayne by breaking all the stereo types he held of local police departments. Wayne believed that the case was resolved because of Chris' loyalty and dedication to the job. Following the accident, Wayne had notified Chris. Wayne had to see if maybe a third party, who knew nothing about his past, yet had experience with criminal investigations could see something that Wayne might be missing. Possibly evidence that might suggest that there was something personal here that Wayne had overlooked. He figured that *if* his suspicions were correct, there might be circumstantial evidence to support Wayne's claim and, if so, he would have to figure out how to pass this off as strictly an accident to the smartest police officer he knew, Ann. To him, it was the only way to be sure.

His thoughts came dangerously close to backfiring. Wayne discovered from Chris' reactions that his story was more transparent than he realized. Chris was not convinced that this was caused by some random act; he had the feeling that Wayne wasn't disclosing pertinent information.

"Come on Wayne!" Chris said, becoming irritable. "You don't think I'm buying that do you? There is something you're not telling me. I can't help you if you can't be completely honest with me!"

"I swear to you Chris! I don't know anyone that would want to do this to me." Wayne really couldn't imagine that the accident was in any way connected with his past. His past was over long ago. Surely they wouldn't be after him now? Would they?

******

Ann and the boys had planned to visit Ann's family out of state. Wayne, who was still in considerable pain with his injury, didn't feel up to traveling, so opted to remain behind. He informed Ann that the peace and quiet would do him some good and allow him to get caught up on some work as well. Shortly after Ann left, Wayne sat down to get started on some proposals for work, when he heard a knock on the door. He wasn't expecting anyone and was irritated at being interrupted. Wayne peered through the front window just as a green sedan sped away. He then opened the door and noticed a small package at the threshold.

Reluctantly, he picked up the small package and retreated into the house. Curious to see what had been left at his door, Wayne opened the box and found a small cell phone inside with a typed, unsigned note that read, "We know where you are Lucas. When the phone rings, answer it!"

Startled, Wayne grabbed his home phone and called Jack.

"Hello?"

"Jack!" Wayne hollered into the receiver.

"Wayne?"

"Listen. They know we're here!"

"Who?"

"Come on Jack!" Wayne replied with irritation. "You know who! I just received confirmation at my doorstep."

"What is it?" Jack asked

"A small phone with a note demanding that when it rings, I must answer it. What do you think, Jack?"

"Throw it out now!" Jack screamed into the phone. "You know how they play! Get that thing away from your house and you, Wayne!"

Wayne dropped the receiver. Grabbing his crutches and the mysterious cell phone, Wayne went outside to a metal trash can in front of the house. After carefully placing the phone in the can and replacing the lid, Wayne hobbled back into the house.

"Jack! You still there?"

"I'm here."

"Okay. I just threw it outside in the can. You think that'll be okay?"

"I sure hope so, at least until I get there." Jack hung up the phone.

Ten minutes later, Jack let himself into the house. "Wayne!" he hollered.

"Yeah, Jack! In here!"

Jack found Wayne in his study. "You okay, man?"

"Sure," Wayne replied. "It's in the trash can out on the curb. What do you think we ought to do?"

"I'm going to get rid of it for you. I'll be back in a bit, cool?"

"Thanks, man!" Wayne replied. "You think you can come back after?"

"I think so." Jack looked at Wayne with a bit of concern on his face. "I just don't understand what went wrong, Wayne. How could they find us?"

"I don't know. The only thing I can think of is that someone must have followed us."

Wayne was wondering how this all could be happening so suddenly. First the accident, which very well could have simply been that, then this. He knew that it was no longer simply a bad chain of events. Somehow, they knew he was alive and they had found him.

Suddenly, there was an explosion from outside. Looking out the front window, Jack could see that the only damage was to the trash can. It had fallen over and the lid had come off.

"Well Wayne," Jack said as he continued to watch out the window. "The good news is that it was a very small bomb which tells me they only wanted to scare you. Probably a warning to let you know they know where you live."

Wayne was grateful his wife was not here to see this. Should there be any further damage, he would have to conceal it before Ann returned home.

"Doesn't mean they know about you, Jack" Wayne informed his friend. "Maybe you ought to lay low for a while until we figure out what's going on."

"Where is Ann?" Jack inquired.

"I took her to the airport. She should be getting to her mom's house soon. I'll let you know when she calls."

Wayne was relieved that Ann was somewhere safe. She would call him as soon as she arrived, which should be any time now.

After arriving at her family's home, Ann phoned Wayne to tell him that she and the boys had arrived safely. "Andrew did very well, honey! I was actually surprised but your boys definitely have your patience! I thought I was going to lose my mind with the delay on our luggage!" She laughed

Wayne tried to laugh with her but found it difficult. He knew that she would be able to detect the strain in his voice.

"Wayne? Honey, what's wrong? Did something happen?" she asked worriedly.

"No, it's alright! Just a few minor complications with the medication I am on," he lied.

Because he was not ready to disclose his past to Ann, Wayne thought it best not to reveal the day's excitement until absolutely necessary. He knew that the package would create undue worry in her and her first reaction would be to take the next flight home. It was important to Wayne that Ann spend time with her family. Besides, there was nothing she could do about it.

"The pain medication seems to be taking effect. I better let you go honey so I can lie down, okay?"

"Ah, honey!" Ann said. "I feel so bad for leaving you when you're trying to recover. Do you want me to leave the boys with Mom and come back home?"

"No, honey, stay with your parents, I insist! They want to spend time with you and the boys, so let them! Besides, Jack is here with me, and wants to assure you that he is taking care of me. Actually, he's helping me get everything I need so I don't have to try to get around the house. No worries, honey!"

"Okay. But you will call me every day to let me know how you are doing, right?" Ann asked him.

Ann stayed with her family for the next seven days, calling Wayne on a regular basis, checking on his status.

Now, all Wayne had to do was figure out who had sent the present and what their next move might be. He would deal with Ann's questions later.

⁂⁂⁂⁂⁂⁂

Ann had never left Wayne for so long, and she was feeling very helpless without him. His current condition with his leg concerned her, and although she knew that he was certainly capable of taking care of himself, she couldn't help but feel that being there would allow her to make sure that he wasn't overdoing activity while his leg was trying to heal.

She knew how lucky he was to have sustained the injuries he did without losing his leg. The surgeries that he had undergone exposed him to infection if he didn't take especially good care and follow all directions. The re-setting of his leg also placed him in a high risk category for permanent disability.

That night, Ann was helping her mother with dinner. Taking advantage of their alone time, Ann thought it the right time to share her concerns.

"Mom, I'm really worried about Wayne."

"What's the matter, honey?"

"I'm just worried about Wayne, Mom. I love him so much and I guess I'm worried that he won't be still and allow himself to heal properly. I'm sure you think I'm over-reacting and I probably am."

Ann smiled at her mother, "He once asked me if I would love him for the rest of his life. I told him 'No, I will love you for the rest of mine.' Pretty sappy, huh?"

"Hey! We all need a bit of romance in our lives! That's wonderful, honey! I wish your dad would have thought of that!" Her mom let out a chuckle.

Her mother was referring to Ann's stepdad who had been a member of their family for many years. He was the only real father Ann had ever known and she loved him a great deal.

"Tell you what, Mom. I'll talk to Dad and slap some romance back into his demeanor for you!" Ann said, laughing.

"Oh, yeah! Good luck with that!"

Ann always felt much better about things after talking to her mom, or even her siblings for that matter. Anytime she had what she considered a tragedy, she would call her mom and sometimes even her sister receiving the comfort and support she could always count on. Ann and her sister, Yvonne, were always very close even after she moved across the United States with her career. She worked now for the government and spent much of her time traveling. She, her husband, and their children spent time in Europe and parts of Asia experiencing various cultures and learning various languages. So, when Ann and Yvonne spent time together, with or without their mother, it was always too short. Even when they spoke on the phone, Ann never wanted their conversations to end. Ann traveled back home to visit her mother as much as possible as their mother too had a hard time with missing Yvonne. It was important to Ann to make every attempt to help her mother. Spending time with her, she felt, was one of the only things she could do.

"Thank you so much for being my mother!" Ann hugged her mom, smiling.

"I think I said that to him because I thought, maybe if I was to outlive him, that loving him for the rest of my life meant loving him for an eternity."

"Honey," her mother said to her gently, "that's a beautiful story!"

"Mom, I know this is going to sound crazy, but I did my own investigation of the accident that Wayne was in and I have a feeling that Wayne isn't telling me something. The accident he was in involved more than one vehicle and when I went to look at our car, even I could see that someone hit him more than once on the side of his car, making it appear almost deliberate. I just have a very bad feeling that Wayne is hiding something from me and I'm not sure why. I can't tell if I'm reading too much into this or if I'm feeling this way because I'm not home with him."

"I'm sure that's all it is."

Together, they let time pass while watching a movie to get their minds off of Wayne. Forty-five minutes later, the phone rang. Ann grabbed the phone and shouted, "Wayne! What's wrong?"

"It's okay, baby. I just called to tell you goodnight," Wayne responded with a warm chuckle.

"I'll be fine, my love. You get some sleep as well. I will call you tomorrow, okay?"

"I can't wait to get home, Wayne. I love you so very much! You made a promise to me that I will always hold you to, you know that right?"

"Which one is that?"

"That we are going to grow old together and sit in our rocking chairs on the front porch, remember? We also promised that we would die on the same day. I'm holding you to that for the rest of our lives. You know that don't you?" Although she appeared to be joking, there was a tension in her voice.

"You know I will always do my best to fulfill any promise we ever made together!" With that, they both said their goodbyes and hung up.

He worried about her a great deal and wanted her to come home more than anything in the world. He knew that he could not tell her the truth behind the "accident" because it would create a question in her regarding his honesty and integrity. Since his feelings for her were more than sincere, he knew for certain that losing her was not a possibility any more than losing his boys would be.

Friday October 3 1983

He was at work running his routine "assembly line" welding duties when he looked up from his current project. Normally, Lucas would receive a light 'tap' on his shoulder to let him know that it was either break time or time to go home for the day. On this particular day, he happened to look up from his work and glance toward the entrance door into the warehouse. That was when he saw that police officer walking toward him. He knew immediately that the officer was looking for him, although he could never say exactly why. The cop had a white clergyman's collar showing above his parka making Lucas' heart skip a beat from dread.

The officer approached him reluctantly.

"Are you Mr. Cavallari? The officer asked.

"Yes sir," Lucas replied, anticipating bad news.

"And you're wife's name is Kay Cavallari?" he inquired

"That's right. Why?" he asked.

"Did she drive a 1979 Toyota? Michigan plates?"

"Yes sir," Lucas replied. He could feel his knees weakening and grabbed the closest chair to sit down.

"Sir, I hate to be the one to tell you this, but we believe your wife and another individual were involved in an accident. Her vehicle was found on the side of the road. Sir, we need you to come down to the morgue to identify the bodies."

As if in an echoing tunnel, Wayne could not believe what he was hearing. His Kay was dead? How could that be possible? He just spoke to her last night! They were arguing about the cause of the divorce. She was trying to convince him that she would never see this Louie person again. Maybe if he had only believed her, she would still be alive. She wanted to get together with him the following morning to talk about their marriage, but he refused telling her that he didn't want to risk missing anymore work.

"There was another person in the car with her or was there a second vehicle. I don't understand," Lucas said.

"There were two bodies in your wife's car, a man and a woman. I'm not even sure if it was your wife in the car. I found no reports indicating the the car might be stolen. So, unless you know if she loaned it out to someone else, maybe?" the officer asked him.

"No. She never lent her car out. I'm pretty sure she would have told me since we were supposed to get together for dinner tonight. Did you find her purse in the car?"

"The damage to the car was extensive, and the bodies were unidentifiable, which is why we need your help at the morgue. As far as any identification, most of the personal property was completely destroyed. The car was badly burned up in the fire." The officer was telling him. "Because the vehicle was registered to your wife, I need you to come with me to see if you can identify one or both of the bodies."

When Lucas arrived at the morgue, he saw a small framed body on a gurney covered with a sheet. The gurney next to the first had a silhouette of a larger body also covered.

"I must tell you. Both bodies were badly disfigured from the fire. We were able to recover some of the personal belongings which we will need you to claim, but no picture identification was found. Just let me know when you're ready."

"I'm as ready as I can be, go ahead."

After pulling back the sheet, Lucas could not believe what he saw. There lay his Kay badly disfigured. Her face and hair were burned almost beyond recognition. With tears in his eyes, he pulled the sheet further back, just enough to see the familiar birthmark on her right bicep, he then picked up her left hand and saw that she was still wearing the wedding ring he gave her.

Oddly, there was a slight feeling of pride when he saw the ring. He supposed it gave him that ounce of encouragement that, they might have had a chance if she were alive. Maybe she was with Louie because she really was intending on getting rid of him once and for all. Although he did still feel anger and jealousy at her for being unfaithful, he knew that he would love his Kay forever. The divorce proceedings could now stop in their tracks and his marriage with her could continue.

Yes sir," he said with a shaky voice, dropping his head away. He couldn't bear to look anymore. "That's her."

"Are you absolutely certain?" the officer asked. "Forgive me, but I have to be sure."

"Yes I'm certain!" Lucas shouted. "What the hell else do you want from me?"

"Okay, I'm sorry sir. You gonna be alright?" The officer asked him.

"Yeah, thanks. You want me to look at the other one now?"

The officer pulled back the sheet from the other body. Sure enough, it was Louie, the guy that Kay was trying to break it off with.

"That's Louie Camboni, officer. Kay was having an affair with him."

"Hell of a way to find out, I'm so sorry," the officer replied, "You said she was supposed to be breaking things off with, what did you mean by that?"

"Yeah. She told me that she was afraid of him and that he had threatened her life. She didn't have a chance to get real specific though. Actually, I told her she was probably just being paranoid and that if she didn't stop seeing him she would lose me. You ever had a case like this before? I mean with a married individual and her lover getting killed in the middle of an affair?"

"I can't say that I have." The officer seemed interested now.

"We will be looking into this a bit further. Do you know if there were actual threats made to your wife?"

"All Kay ever said was that she was afraid of Louie. She never gave me any exact quotes of him telling her he was going to kill her or anything. If that will be all, sir, I really want to go home now." Wayne headed for the door.

"You gonna be okay?" The officer asked him.

"Eventually, I suppose I will." Lucas replied. Shoulders slumped, Lucas walked out into the daylight.

The officer's name was Michael Santino. Michael had transferred from New York a number of years ago to relocate to Michigan. His goal was to become chief of police and help Guido take over Michigan as well. Now that Louie, Antonio and Kay were all taken care of, all Michael had to do was find the pictures and documents and the entire state would be theirs.

Michael knew that Lucas had information on the senators running for office and that information was pertinent to the Cosa Nostra. With the pictures and inside information they had, Guido's family would have full control over two states, now, offering permanent security to their wealth and power, a goal that Michael had been helping Guido with most of his adult life. He would stop at nothing to make sure that he gathered this information from Lucas, and now, it was simply a matter of finding it and getting it back to Guido. The Bone Breakers, too, were looking for any evidence on the senators which could also work to Michaels benefit, getting him into office like he always planned. In order to move forward, they would have to get rid of Lucas.

Following the identification process, Lucas headed straight for the scene of the accident where he discovered not one, but two sets of tracks on the icy road. If this was an act of Frankie's boys, Lucas had to assume that they would be out for him next. He was sure that Michael did not know that Lucas was aware of his involvement with the Cosa Nostra, but he couldn't bank on that assumption. Having no time to consider grieving over Ann, Lucas made every attempt to focus on what was important, getting himself out of a potentially bad situation. He was very well aware that Kay did not end her relationship with Louie as she said she was going to and focusing on *that* made him a bit more capable of focusing on the task at hand.

Lucas immediately contacted his friend and business partner, Tony.

"Tony, it's time," Lucas told him. "Go to my parents and get the plan going like we discussed. I'll meet you tonight. You know where."

The connection was broken and Lucas headed back to his house to gather the necessary equipment.

Lucas and Tony had grown up together and both became involved in motorcycles at a young age. Tony had a difficult childhood making him callous and unsociable. When the boys first met, Lucas was riding his bicycle around the neighborhood when another kid raced to catch up to him.

"Hey", the kid said to him, "you live around here?"

"Yeah," Lucas said. "Who are you?"

"I'm Tony. My family just moved in around the block. Come on! I'll show you my new house. What's your name?" Tony asked him.

"I'm Lucas! Let's go, I'll race ya!"

From there, Lucas and Tony became inseparable. Lucas spent much of his childhood helping Tony stay away from his home. They would run errands for Tony's mother when she needed them to, but would avoid his father at all cost. His father was a heavy drinker and would beat his wife and child often.

As teenagers, they both saved their money in order to build their own motorcycles. They began spending much of their time at a local salvage yard bartering for parts whenever possible. When it wasn't possible, they would gather the agreed amount to purchase the part they needed. Over time, they were able to gather enough parts to complete the construction of their first motorcycle and spent their summer months taking turns learning to ride. Eventually, they both became dedicated members of the Bone Breakers.

As the best friend of the club's most reliable informant, Tony had made a lifelong commitment to stick by Lucas no matter what. So when it started looking as if the club and the mafia might come after Luke, Tony committed to doing whatever possible to save his friend.

Tony always really liked Kay and was shocked at her affair with Louie. He spoke with her about it only once, but she wouldn't provide him with any explanation as to why she would do something like that to Luke. When Tony found out whom Kay was seeing, he warned her to get away from him as quickly as possible. She refused, so, Tony had no choice but to warn Luke about it. When Kay had gone to Luke for help, Tony knew that things were going to go bad rather quickly. Although he never anticipated the boys killing her quite this soon, Tony knew that staging his and Lucas' death was the only possible solution to avoid the retaliation that was inevitable.

Two days after Kay's death, Lucas and Tony had set the stage for an explosion at the warehouse. They were both expected to be working late on a last minute shipment when the tanks blew up demolishing the entire plant.

Monday October 9, 1983

Guido answers his phone, "Yeah?"

"Guido! It's Frankie"

"Yeah, Frankie! What do ya want?"

"There was an explosion last night at the factory that Lucas and Tony work at. According to Michael, the two of them were there. The job is already done for us! Isn't that great news?" Frankie was so excited. Now, he would be in Guido's good graces for sure!

Even though Frankie was a member of the family, as Guido's nephew, he had gotten himself into some serious trouble in the past. Guido had stepped up for him so that Frankie would not be ex-communicated from the family and took Frankie under his wing. Frankie basically lived his life trying to prove his worth to his uncle Guido. Every decision Frankie made seemed to leave him feeling incompetent. If this situation turned out to be one that actually worked in Frankie's favor, his efforts might prove his capabilities not only to Guido, but to the entire family as well.

"How do you know they were actually there, Frankie?" Guido asked.

"Apparently, there were two bodies found in the warehouse. Tony and Lucas arranged with their employer to be there working on some job and the security badge reader confirmed they were there. Their badges were also found among the rubble in the warehouse. According to Mike, their dental records confirmed that it was them. The point is, they're dead Guido! Now they're all taken care of!"

"Yeah, okay but don't let your guard down, Frankie! I'm not so sure I'm buyin' it! See if you can't get a hold of Michael to confirm it. Then, and only then, will I feel better about it!"

"All right, Guido. I will call you back once I find something out."

Two days later, Frankie had called back to report that the evidence found was more than enough to identify the bodies of Lucas and Tony and that they were both reported deceased by Michael and the police department. Death certificates had been issued.

November 1985

"Mom?" Wayne said into the receiver.

"Lu…um…Wayne? Is that you?" Maggie asked. She was still having a hard time remembering his new name. Actually, she didn't much like it. She knew him as Luke or Lucas and that was that.

"Be careful, Mom. I'm fine. I thought I would let you know that I have a place all set up for you and Dad. You're both coming, right?"

"Oh my gosh, honey!" Maggie shouted, "Of course we are! We'll be there in two days!"

Wayne's parents had been waiting for what seemed like an eternity to hear from their youngest boy. Maggie and Tom were asked more than a year ago to be patient. He would contact them as soon as he could.

Now, that time had finally come and they were more than ready for it. Maggie had the bags packed and ready to go for all these months, desperately waiting for her son to notify her and Tom to get out of this God-for-saken state they were in and move closer to her son. The only thing they knew for sure was that their boy had remarried and had plans to start a family of his own. But that information had come to them through Tony or rather, Jack, and Maggie had a hard time believing anything Jack had to say. After all, it *had* to be his fault that her Lucas was in this situation. She never really liked that kid. Then again, she didn't like any of Luke's friends, none of them were good enough for her favorite son.

Anxiously waiting for this day, both gathered only what they considered to be the essentials, trying desperately to get on the road as quickly as possible. Then, the moving company was notified to pack up the rest of their belongings and deliver it to their new residence once they arrived.

She already had a pretty good idea of where they were going to live since they both were very familiar with the state. Wayne had made arrangements, and she knew that he would place them in one of her favorite areas. Wayne knew them both very well and, he would abide by her wishes. She and Tom had vacationed in Arizona many times in their past, making things that much easier for all of them.

This day had finally arrived and both secretly hoped that their Wayne would not be disappointed. When they saw each other, it was as if no time had actually passed. They hugged and spent their first day catching up with their stories.

Wayne didn't discuss his past, but instead shared stories of his life with his new wife, Ann. He told them about how the two of them had met, how they had become the best of friends, and how they rode together. They shared pictures of their vacations and told them about building their home and their future plans.

Ann knew that his parents were living in his home state and because they never had the opportunity to take a trip there, she hadn't yet met them. In all honesty, Wayne had no intention of ever returning to that state, not wanting to jeopardize his death to the Cosa Nostra and the Bone Breakers.

Nervous about the introduction, Ann was in her room trying on different outfits. "Honey, you look great!" Wayne said when he walked in the room.

"Are you sure?" Ann asked nervously. "I want everything to be perfect, Wayne!"

"It is, you are! Besides, they're already here waiting to meet you. Come on, let's go downstairs. I'm afraid if you change again, you're gonna tell me we need to go shopping because none of your clothes are perfect enough!" Wayne was making fun of her, and she knew it.

"Actually," Ann began

"I don't think so, kiddo! Now come on!"

He grabbed her hand and led her out of the room to the top of the stairs to make a grand entrance. Both Maggie and Tom were taken by her beauty and could see the unmistakable happiness in their son's eyes.

Following the proper introductions, they all sat down to the dinner table while Ann served. Everything tasted wonderful. Wayne couldn't help but beam with delight whenever he looked at his beautiful new wife. He never imagined his life so perfect.

After everyone had finished eating and were all setting back in their chairs to begin conversing about the latest news in all of their lives, Ann stood to clear the table. Finished her task, she returned to the dining room.

"I have something I would like to share with all of you."

Everyone stopped their conversation to look at Ann.

"Go ahead, dear," Maggie said, "We're listening."

Feeling herself becoming embarrassed, Ann stood next to the table, "First, I want to thank you both for coming. I cannot tell you what an absolute pleasure it is to finally meet you! You're son means everything in the world to me, and with or without the agreement of matrimony, I plan to spend the rest of my life at his side." Ann had the most beautiful smile Wayne had ever seen. "Also," Ann continued, "I went to the doctor this morning, Wayne. I was going to tell you earlier, but I thought we should include your parents."

"What is it, honey?" Wayne asked with a look of concern on his face.

"I already called my family to tell them. I hope you don't mind, honey. So this means you aren't the first to know about it. We're going to have a baby!" Ann announced.

"Oh my God!" Maggie exclaimed, covering her mouth. "When?"

"In about seven months from now." Ann replied

"Is everything okay? I mean, how are you feeling? Do you need to rest?"

" I'm fine!" Ann replied with a laugh. "Fit as a fiddle!"

They all had gathered around Ann who was standing at the head of the table.

"What about work?" Tom asked her, referring to her police patrol.

"I plan to work into my fifth or sixth month and then take maternity leave after that, provided everything runs smoothly."

"Wow!" Wayne said. "I'm going to be a dad!"

He never expected this in fact, he had never really wanted children, but now that he knew it would actually happen, his thoughts on the subject seemed to change. They hadn't even discussed the possibility of children with their current work schedules.

That night, the two of them found themselves talking about her pregnancy and work. "I don't want to take off too early, Wayne." Ann said. "Let me stay at work until the doctor feels I should begin maternity leave. That way, maybe it will help the time pass and keep my mind off the nausea!"

"Really? Is it bad?"

"You know how I get in the car? Yeah! It's a lot like that!"

Ann was notorious for getting motion sickness. Their first year together, for Wayne's birthday at the end of March, they went on a trip to Mexico. Ann thought it would be a great idea to take Wayne deep-sea fishing. Thinking nothing of it, and because she had never been out on the ocean before, it never occurred to Ann that she might get sick.

The following months preparations ran smoothly, with Ann maintaining her nausea faithfully through the eight month. The delivery went well, quick and without any notable complications.

Phillip, their new baby boy was born in the beginning of July.

Although Wayne didn't see it, everyone thought he looked exactly like his father.

Ann's mom and sister attended the birth and stayed with Ann for the next two weeks to make sure everything was taken care of for her while Ann got a chance to rest.

Tom and Maggie couldn't have been more proud. Their son had proven himself capable of completely turning his life around; he was now a successful businessman and a proud husband and father. They both adored their new daughter-in-law and couldn't get enough of their grandson. Ann was absolutely perfect for their son. He seemed much happier after losing Kay.

Wayne was proving to both his parents that they were wrong when they assumed that he had gotten himself in too deep and would never be able to leave his past behind him.

New York City

Guido had received a phone call from Frankie in Michigan.

"Hey Guido! Remember Lucas Cavalleri?"

"Yeah." Guido said with disgust

"I found out that he is still alive! You were right! I had one of my employees, Laurie, watching his parents just out of curiosity and, wouldn't you know it, they packed everything up and moved to Arizona. But they did it, all of a sudden like. So, Laurie followed them and, there was Lucas! He's married now, isn't that cozy?"

"Ok…dam it, Frankie! I thought maybe there was something to that explosion so many years ago. I thought you said the death was confirmed? How can that be if he is still alive? This is a huge problem for us, Frankie! Get two of your best out there to take care of this, Frankie. But have them hold back for a while until we get more information. We certainly don't want to miss this time and I don't want to raise any suspicion!" Then, Guido reconsidered, "Oh, hell, Frankie. Never mind. I'll get two of my best out there. I got a couple of guys in mind"

"Who are you thinking of sending?" Frankie wanted to know.

"Sal and Ramon" Guido told him, "You remember Sal, don't you?"

"Oh sure. But who's Ramon?" Frankie asked him.

"New guy. He was sent to me by your father. Outsider, but very reliable. He's proven himself to everyone. Pulled a job that I'll have to tell you about some other time. Anyway, I'll let you know when they'll be out there. Expect them within the next forty-eight hours."

Frankie hung up and sat in wonderment at the fact that Lucas could still be alive. Nice trick, what he did with the dental impressions on the corpses. He supposed it was possible that his buddy Tony could still be alive as well, if he was, Frankie would find out.

******

The next few months were spent focusing on their family life. Ann went back to work and Tom and Maggie spent most of their time with their grandson.

A year had passed and Wayne had been spending most of his time working and with Phillip. Everything seemed to be going quite well until one evening when Jack paid them a visit.

Jack had informed Wayne that things were getting a bit heated once again.

"What do you mean, Jack?" Wayne wanted to know.

"Do you remember Alex?" Jack asked him.

"Of course" Wayne replied.

"Alex was found dead this morning. He was shot in the back."

"Jesus!" Wayne exclaimed. "Any idea who might have done it?"

"Yep. And I think you know the answer to that question, Wayne."

"After all this time? Come on, Jack! Why would they come after him now? And how would they know he's still alive?"

Recalling back to their past, Wayne remembered how Alex had gotten wrapped up in the idea of leaving the life and starting his own family. When the family agrees to someone leaving, if they allowed them to live, there was no chance of that person becoming successful in that state. The mafia would see to that. Instead of leaving, Alex decided to start doing business with their rival club, drug deals, selling weapons, a dangerous way of life for Alex.

"I guess he ran because he was living here when they found him."

"Okay, so what are you thinking, Jack?"

"That they're awful close, Wayne. I just think we should be careful. I was hoping that you might consider moving to New Mexico or Texas."

"Are you kidding me, Jack? I am not going to spend the rest of my life uprooting my family and running scared. We left the life behind us. They can't possibly know that we are here or even alive. My parents are here now, and this is the life that I want. Nope, forget it Jack, I'm stayin' right where I'm at."

"Okay, Wayne, just watch you're back. I'm scared they might be on to us, that's all." Jack said.

Wayne walked Jack out to his car and thanked him for the information. He didn't really believe that the Cosa Nostra would be back and looking for him again, but Jack's words had an impact on him all the same.

Within six months of Phillips birth, Ann was pregnant with their second son, Andrew. After his birth, Ann received the promotion she had worked so hard for, and as a result she was working practically around the clock. Wayne was spending most of his time after work studying for exams that he was taking to advance his own career.

Wayne and Ann could not imagine themselves any luckier than to have each other and the most beautiful boys anyone could dream of parenting.

They both agreed that public schools were not the best choice, so they enrolled them both into a special school program that would give them better scholarship opportunities as well as a more in-depth education. The school they chose was very well known, and they had the ability to transfer anywhere they chose. Although it would be difficult for Ann to be without them, she wanted nothing but the best for them.

While making the necessary arrangements and sending them off to military school, Ann had obtained a sergeant position with the department. As such, that September she was called out of state to assist with a mass casualty incident that had caused virtually the entire coastal region of the state damage from a hurricane. Her role there was as a volunteer, and it was her duty to oversee others and to assist with the accommodation of survivors with the necessary equipment. There was no telling how long she would be gone; in fact it wouldn't be out of the question to prepare to be away for months. Wayne helped Ann gather the necessary provisions such as food, water, and emergency equipment to take with her as the extent of the damage was not yet determined.

As Ann was pulling out to leave, Wayne ran out of the garage waving at her to stop. Running up to the car, Ann jumped out and Wayne grabbed her in a tight hug.

"I am so proud of you honey!" Wayne told her. "You have no idea how much I already miss you and how much I love you!"

Ann looked up into his eyes and replied, "Not as much as I love you! I want you home when I get back and stay out of the hospital!" she said with a laugh, referring to the last time she had left town following his accident. Wayne hollered back at her as he waved goodbye, "You're not getting rid of me that easy!" He turned to walk into the house.

As Ann headed out for a long drive, she was thinking about her boys and her husband, amazed at how much she missed them already. After a long two hours, Ann could stand it no longer so she called Wayne to talk.

"Hi sweetie!" Ann said quietly into the phone. "I just want to tell you that I love you so very much. I think I might just turn around right now and head back. I don't want to do this anymore, honey!"

"Oh, baby!" Wayne replied with much sincerity. "I miss you too, but you have to do this. I know how important it really is to you. Everything will be fine." Jokingly, he said, "You're the one that has to deal with my separation anxiety so somehow, I think that's your problem. Let's see, what can I do to get you to come home early this time?" He laughed and she could picture that dreamy smile on his face, the same one that attracted her in the very beginning so many years ago.

"I love you so much, Wayne! Please don't let it consume you, okay? I will be constantly thinking about you and will be home as soon as I can! Remember, you have to come back to me, right?"

"Of course, honey. And I promise that I will always come back to you and only you! I love you."

Because of the damage from the storm, the only lights along the highway were those run by generators, gas stations were unable to pump gas, and grocery stores were completely shut down. The situation was far worse than she had expected.

After a couple of weeks of handing out supplies, all personnel had pushed themselves beyond the point of exhaustion, including Ann. Even though she and Wayne had done their best to make the necessary accommodations, much of the food she had brought along had gone bad as the ice in the cooler had melted. She was losing a considerable amount of weight, something that she was too small to be able to afford.

Then one evening, she received a call from her husband's phone.

"Hi baby! Are you okay?" she asked anxiously. It was Wayne's friend, Jack, on the other end.

"Hi Ann. It's Jack," Jack replied with a strange tone in his voice. Ann wondered why on earth Jack would be calling on Wayne's phone.

41

"Jack? Are you okay? What's wrong? Where is Wayne?!" Ann asked, now at the point of hysteria. Although she knew she was jumping to conclusions, this was highly out of the ordinary as Wayne would never let anyone use his phone to call her, not even as a joke.

"No, Ann, I'm not." He let out a heavy sigh. "I've got some bad news."

Ann could feel her heart rate increasing.

Pausing, Jack continued, "I guess I'll just say it. Wayne was in an accident. It's real bad."

"What? Jack! What are you saying? How bad? What the hell are you talking about?" Ann's face was completely flushed. A few of the other officers gathered around, placing their hands on Ann as they tried to calm her. At this point, all they knew was that she had just received news from someone, yet no one knew who or what about.

"A truck turned left into him while he was on his motorcycle. There was no time for Wayne to respond, Ann. He hit the front end of the truck, the impact was so hard that the spindle was broken leaving the truck un-drivable. A witness says Wayne was doing about forty-five miles per hour and had no time to stop. The drivers of the truck ran off, but the witness was able to give a good description of both men. The boys don't know a thing yet. You need to get home as soon as possible. The doctor doesn't think he's going to make it, Ann."

As she hung up the phone, Ann fell back into a chair, the other officers running up to her side. Her face went completely pale; she buried it in her hands and began to shake uncontrollably. Suddenly, she let out a terrible scream.

Wayne made Phillip and Andrew laugh effortlessly. He did everything possible to make sure that the boys were having the time of their lives. Although well disciplined by both their parents, the father-son relationship they had was closer than Ann had ever dreamed possible, since she herself grew up without a dad. The boys knew that their parents were not only very happy together and had been all their lives, but also the best of friends. As Wayne made the boys laugh, they made each other laugh all the same. During their childhood, neither of the boys could remember his parents actually fighting. Sure, they argued from time to time, but their arguments never resulted in anything more than the both of them laughing in the end. Following a particular argument, they watched their parents step away from each other only to return with shared jokes.

Neither Andrew nor Phillip ever questioned his parents' happiness until the day their father was hit. Although they had seen their parents argue over the years, they had never seen their mom as depressed and withdrawn as she had become following that horrible phone call. With the news that their father was in the hospital, the school had received the call about Wayne's accident, sending the boys home immediately.

Escorted by their grandmother, Phillip and Andrew waited outside for their mother who was standing at Wayne's side in the Intensive Care Unit.

As Ann walked out to the waiting room, Andrew placed his arms on her shoulders and gave her a hug.

"Oh, Andrew! Oh my God, honey! Phillip, when did you two get here?"

"We just got here, honey," Ann's mother said as she walked up to embrace her daughter.

"Oh Mom! Thank you so much for being here!"

"Where's Dad?" Phillip asked

"He's in the hospital room, honey," Ann told him. "You can't go in there. No children are allowed in that section of the hospital."

At that moment, the nurse walked into the waiting room, indicating that the doctor wanted the family for a meeting in the "cry" room. Ann motioned for the boys to come back into the room. Phillip and Andrew could both feel their heart rates increase from fear.

"Mom! Don't let them kill my dad, okay?"

"Baby, why would you say that?" Ann asked her son with concern.

"I saw it in a movie once. The guy was hit by a big truck and they didn't want to let him live so they shut the machines off and he died. I guess the machines were his breath. Just don't let them say he won't make it, Mom! I love my dad, and I don't want those people to take his breath from him!"

Ann's mother grabbed Phillip to console him. "I'll sit out here with the boys, honey. You go on ahead with the Moore's, okay?"

"Ok, Mom, thanks," Ann replied with a weak voice. With her shoulders slumped she turned to go into the room and await the inevitable.

The doctor had indicated that the damage was just too severe and Wayne would not be capable of ever regaining consciousness. Wayne was now diagnosed as medically brain dead.

"You're saying that I should pull the plug and let my husband die?" Ann asked the doctor.

"I am saying that with the extent of the damage, there is no possible way that I can tell you what you want to hear. Your husband will never fully recover. Nor do I expect him to live without the machines. It is my suggestion that you abide by the wishes in his will and let him go. Of course, the decision is yours to make."

Following the meeting the family went back into the room to gather around Wayne's bed. Ann knew that she could not put this off any longer as she watched Wayne receiving assistance from the machines. The monitors indicating that his breathing and life were both maintained by artificial means, she question whether he was able to feel anything and, if so, if any sensations were of pain. The thought of that was too much for her to handle.

The attending nurse explained to the family that she was going to give Wayne an injection to make him more comfortable. She explained that the medication would prevent him from experiencing any sensations of suffocation and that he would actually drift off into a deep sleep as his heart stopped. Ann politely thanked her as she administered the injection. Slowly, Wayne's breathing became less labored and more and more shallow. Suddenly, Ann turned to the nurse and screamed.

" Wait! I want to take it back! Start the machines again. He's not ready to go, see? He's still breathing! I can't let him go. I need him too much! Please! Start the machines again!" Ann fell onto Wayne, crying hysterically while holding on to his shoulders.

The nurse approached Ann's mother-in-law and whispered, "Is she going to be okay? Do you think she might need something to help calm her?"

"That might be a good idea. I don't think anyone can fathom the pain she is going through right now. She'll make it. We're just gonna have to give her some time." Ann's mother watched all the while with concern for her precious daughter wanting only to take the pain away.

****

At the funeral, two days later, Ann had reconsidered attending. She secretly hoped that if she didn't show, maybe the funeral would not happen and all this would go away. Although some attempted to console her immediately following her arrival, others had shown concern for her being late. Maggie stood as she approached, grabbed her hand, and hugged her. Ann turned to Tom.

"Tom," Ann said to her father-in-law, "please make this go away. I love him so much! I miss him, and I thought that if I didn't show up, maybe Wayne might come back to me. I'm so sorry for being late! I didn't mean any disrespect. Will you forgive me?" She slowly sat down, knowing that no matter what she did, the funeral was going to happen.

"I know, baby!" Tom replied as he grabbed Ann's shoulder. "We all have to somehow learn to accept this for Lu...I mean, Wayne."

Ann turned to look at Tom with a hint of questioning just as the reverend began his sermon.

At the beginning of the sermon, Ann became curious about what Tom had just said.

"Oh, well," she thought, "he's just upset and thinking of something else, I'm sure." But Ann didn't believe her own justification.

After the ceremony, the reverend invited the family to say a few words on Wayne's behalf. Following the presentation of each of his siblings and both his parents, Ann stood in front of the entire congregation to express her true feelings for Wayne. Holding up a piece of paper, she looked at the audience with hesitation and began,

"I thought it best to help you all understand that Wayne was the one man in my life, my absolute everything! He was my best friend and the father of my children, he loved the three of us with all his heart and soul. Before the boys were born, he handed me a framed poem that he had written for me, so I thought this an appropriate time to share it with all of you. You know, I haven't stopped reading this for years. I had it memorized until, all of a sudden, I couldn't remember a word of it!" With a smirk, she paused to wipe the tears from her eyes.

"What I would do if I found my soul mate." She paused to catch her breath and continued reading. "Kiss her in front of my friends, trust her over everyone else, and tell her she looks beautiful. I would look her in the eyes when I talk to her, tell her stupid jokes to make her laugh and even let her mess with my hair. I would walk around with her to no place in particular, include her in the things I do, and when she cries, I will do whatever necessary to make her smile. I will forgive her for her mistakes and look at her like she is the only woman I see." She paused a second time as she wiped the tears from her face and cleared her throat. "I will tickle her just a little, even when she says 'stop', hold her hand when we are around friends, and if she swears at me, I will tell her that I love her anyway. She will always be welcome to fall asleep in my arms and if I tease her, I will let her tease me back." Ann paused to wipe her eyes. Trying desperately to hold her composure. "I will stay up with her all night when she is sick, watch her favorite movie, kiss her forehead and give her the world. I will always write her letters even when I am not gone, and when she is sad, I will hang out with her and let her know that she is the most important person in the world to me. I will let her take all the photos of me that she wants, I will kiss her in the rain and when I fall in love with her, I will tell her. And when I do tell her, I will love her like I have never loved before. I love you, Ann!" She looked up at the room filled with people and continued in a sobbing voice, "Wayne lived up to every word of this poem. I want you all to know that the motorcycle did not kill him. It was something else and I will not stop until I get to the bottom of what caused my husband's death. I ask that all of you respect that and do not use Wayne's death as a reason to quit riding your own bikes. All of you know that he would disagree with any of you no longer riding. That would break his heart!" With slumped shoulders, she quietly walked out of the room while the rest of the crowd parted for her. No one said a word.

After she returned home, Ann confined herself to her bed for three days keeping her head covered. She wept uncontrollably until she fell asleep, only to awaken and repeat the same actions. The boys let her be as much as they could. She was not willing to eat or drink until one day, she received the only visitor capable of getting through to her. It wasn't until the fourth day following the funeral that Phillip and Andrew's Aunt Yvonne came to visit all the way from Virginia to check on her little sister.

Yvonne arrived without warning, heading immediately to their parents' bedroom.

"Hey sis!" Yvonne whispered to Ann

"Yvonne?" Ann sat up in bed, unable to believe her eyes. They hadn't seen each other in five years.

"Yeah, sweetie! It's me. How ya doin' kiddo?"

"I was really happy, Yvonne! Wayne was everything to me and now, I am supposed to be without him. How am I supposed to do that, Yvonne, how?" Ann began sobbing as Yvonne lay down next to her and hugged her.

"I know, sweetie, I know! But you need to get out of bed and keep living! There's so much out there for you. I know it's hard to see that right now, but you have a whole lot of life left ahead of you. Wayne's death had to be for something and watching you wither away is not it! Those two little boys need you and they have to get back to school!" Yvonne rubbed Ann's arm as she spoke.

"I know. I told everyone at the funeral that I would get to the bottom of his death. I'm just afraid that if I don't find anything, his death will just be an accident. Yvonne, I can't take another 'accident' in my life! This just isn't fair! I'm only forty years old and I don't find any reason to get any older."

"Ah, honey! I will do what I can to help you, you know that don't you?" While watching her little sister, Yvonne could feel her worry growing and wasn't sure what to do about it. Not finding any words for her, Yvonne could only promise to help in any way possible.

Wayne's body was cremated in accordance with his wishes. Ann placed the beautiful urn in their living-room with intentions of spreading his ashes someday. The three went through the motions over the following weeks, barely talking to each other.

Having taken leave from their studies, the boys were to stay home with their mother, to get through this terrible tragedy as a family. Ann was on bereavement leave from work and, although Ann discovered that Phillip seemed to be withdrawn from everything in his world, she could understand and knew that she was guilty of the same thing.

"Phillip, I need to talk to you." Ann said one evening as she entered his room.

"Can you please just leave me alone?" Phillip replied without looking at his mother.

"No, I won't leave you alone. I want to talk to you, honey. We need to talk about your father."

"Mom?" Phillip sat up to look at his mother. His face was streaked with tears and his eyes were swollen and bloodshot. "What do you think really happened to dad? Do you think someone actually did this on purpose?"

"I'm not sure, sweetie." Ann replied with a look of sympathy on her face. "The men who hit your father's motorcycle ran away, so the police are looking for them. We aren't sure yet who they are or why they ran the way they did, but we will find them, honey."

"Do you think they're bad guys, like in the movies?" Phillip asked

"Well, maybe honey. Where are you getting this stuff from, anyway? Is you're friend Scottie telling you this stuff?"

"No. I did watch a real cool movie with Scottie, though. There weren't any bad words, just a bunch of bad guys shooting at good guys. I used to watch those kind of movies with dad all the time. This one time, dad and I were watching a movie that was really cool. It had these spaceship guys in it, and when one of them got hit with a big truck, the doctors had him on a machine that was his breath, that's what dad told me, anyway. Did dad have aliens taking care of him when they took his breath?" Phillip wondered.

"You have *got* to stop watching those kind of movies, Phil." Ann said with a smile. Then, she got serious with him. Holding onto his chin to bring his face up to hers, she looked in his eyes and asked, "You okay, sport? You know you are the man of the house now, right? You're brother and I need you to help take care of us."

"Like dad took care of everybody?" Phillip wanted to know.

"Just like dad did, yes." Ann told him

"Yeah, Mom, I will be okay. Thank you." Phillip laid down to go to sleep. Ann kissed him goodnight and quietly shut the door.

She went to her own room to get herself ready for bed. Entering into the closet, she saw all of Wayne's clothes hanging neatly. She walked up to his group of shirts, wrapped her arm around as many as she could and buried her face in them, trying to get a last whiff of Wayne's beautiful smell. As she stood there, she realized that she had never told him how much she enjoyed the things they all did together. She never mentioned how much she loved to lay her head on his chest and listen to his heart beating. She never told him how much she loved the way he smelled.

Ann began to cry once again as she stood with her face buried in the clothing. Faintly, she heard a noise coming from the doorway of the closet. Startled, she turned to see her youngest boy standing in the doorway with a look of curiosity on his face.

"Mom." Andrew said, "I can't sleep."

"Oh, honey," Ann turned toward him as she wiped her face. Kneeling down in front of him, she said, "What's keeping you from sleeping, darlin'?"

"My dad."

"What do you mean, honey?" Ann asked him.

"He keeps talking to me. I can't go to sleep because he keeps talking."

"You can hear him?" Ann thought maybe Andrew was reverting back to when he was younger and had his imaginary friends.

"Yes. Can't you hear him?"

"Is he talking to you right now?"

"Yes. He doesn't want me to go to sleep."

"Well," Ann thought for a moment, "Why don't you tell him to tell you one of his silly stories? You always liked his stories."

"Okay!" Andrew said, brightening up.

Having been a police officer for so many years, Ann always felt that she handled death quite well. She was the rock solid one at the scene of the accidents that she attended. She never let the death of another frighten or even upset her because she knew that it was never about her. It was about the survivors. This time, however, she was in the position of the survivor and realized that most of the words she used to comfort people really weren't helpful at all. Until now, she couldn't understand what they were going through. Now, she had first hand experience and found that there were no words that could make this horrible nightmare go away.

Not only was she survivor, but so were her two boys. She had no way of knowing what the proper words were for this type of a situation and certainly didn't know if what she was doing was the right thing. She felt completely helpless for the second time in her life. At least, she thought, the loss of her first husband involved her alone, so she could self-absorb into her work. This time, she felt like she never wanted to leave her home again, not as long as she could help it anyway.

Talking with the boys earlier that week, she gave them instruction on how to handle all of this that even she couldn't follow. She said to them both, "When you get angry, yell. When you are sad, cry. And know that, somehow, it will get easier to accept over time."

Then Phillip had said to her, "I just miss my dad so much, Mom, and I'm scared to believe that he's gone. I never imagined that I might have to live without him. I always thought he would be here with me and now that he isn't, I don't know what I'm supposed to do. He wasn't supposed to die, Mom!" Tears began falling down his cheeks.

"I know, honey. But you're supposed to go on living, Phil and keep making your father proud of you. I don't want you closing off to me, your brother or, most importantly, yourself. Your father loved you very,

very much, honey. There was not a moment that went by that he wasn't thinking of all of us." Phillip placed his arms around his mothers' shoulders as she too began to cry. "You will always have a very strong part of your father in you." They hugged for quite sometime, until they both felt that the tears would stop if only for a moment. Ann realized then, and possibly for the first time, how much Phillip looked and acted like his father.

"Do you dream about him, honey?" Ann asked him

"Sometimes. But I don't really remember the dreams I have."

"That's okay. You don't have to. Do you ever feel like he's watching over you?" Ann asked

"Do you mean in heaven?" Phillip asked her.

"Yes. Do you believe that he is an angel now and is watching us?"

"Yes. Is that okay, Mom?" Phillip asked continuing to cry.

"I believe that he is in heaven, Mom." Andrew offered.

"Do you?" Ann asked him.

"Yep. I think he is with Snickers now." Andrew said

Snickers was their dog they had for years. One of the most reliable that Ann had ever had, Snickers developed an intestinal infection and they couldn't get it to reverse. Snickers had died in the middle of the night in his sleep, at least that's what Wayne and Ann told the boys.

"Well, honey." Ann said, "I think you're right. I think that your dad and Snickers are rolling around on the ground laughing and playing." That was what Wayne used to do the minute he walked in the house. He would holler to little Snickers, get down on all fours and tease that dog almost without mercy. He told Ann one time that he did this to make ol' Snick sleep. After they lost him, Wayne had considered getting another dog, but they had never gotten around to doing it. Ann was thinking to herself that, possibly, they could look into that starting tomorrow.

The boys were both looking at her, possibly searching for something more. So Ann looked first at Phil, then at Andy,

"Do you know that I still talk to him?" Ann asked them.

"Me too!" Pipped in Andrew.

"I don't." Phil replied.

"Why not?" Ann asked. "You might want to try just talking to him, like he is your special invisible or imaginary friend."

"I guess he is now, isn't he?" Phillip asked her.

"If you want him to be, honey. I know he would like that."

"Mom," Phillip asked. "do you believe in God and angels?"

"Yes, I suppose I do. I guess I wouldn't talk to your dad if I didn't, huh?" She looked at him with a slight smile on her face.

"I'm glad, Mom. I want dad to be in a good place with God. I want him to be an angel."

"Well, then. I suppose that he is, if that's what you want darlin'."

To this point, Ann had never held much thought in religion. Not that she discounted it, only that she and Wayne were not strong believers in organized faith. At this particular moment, however, she was considering the possibilities of attending a church to, if nothing else, help all of them learn how to believe or accept that Wayne must be in a better place. That a loving sole like his was able to continue on, or maybe to somehow believe that he was waiting for them when their time eventually came.

"Mom?" Phillip asked looking at her with the sweetest little face. She couldn't remember the last time he had looked at her like that. He had such a look of innocence, she was thinking about how much she missed that.

"What is it, honey?"

"I really love you a lot!" Phil said as he threw himself on her with a huge 'bear hug'.

Following the biggest hug she remembered ever having received from him, she looked at Andrew with tears in her eyes. Andrew hugged her just as Phil had done while whispering, "I love you Mom!" into her ear.

✳✳✳✳✳✳

Over the next few months, Ann created her own routine, hoping that if she kept busy, she would distract herself and possibly develop a sense of stability. She opted to make as few changes to her life as possible, feeling that making any concrete decisions would only result in failure.

Ann and the boys were invited to a birthday party for one of Wayne's closest friends, Sam. The three of them felt somewhat out of place initially, but over time began to warm up to the point where they began to mingle among people who Ann recognized from Wayne's past. Others would approach her and introduce themselves as friends of Wayne's from Michigan. After being there for only an hour or two, and while standing close to the bar, a woman approached Ann from behind. Taking notice of the bandage on Ann's shoulder the woman said, "Oh! Did you just get a tattoo?"

Not overly interested in meeting this particular person, Ann replied with, "Yeah."

"What did you get," the woman continued in a giddy, Valley girl voice that immediately grated on Ann's nerves.

"Oh, honey! It's *amazing*!" Ann replied with fabricated glee. "It's a picture of road rash from 'The Cave Creek 540'!"

"Road rash?" the stupid woman inquired. "Why would you get a tattoo of road rash?"

"Because that's the only way to win the race!" Ann replied, again with sarcasm. "Bye-bye!" Ann said to the girl while shooing her away with her hand.

As the woman walked on, oblivious to Ann's demeaning manner, a man standing nearby began to chuckle. Turning to face him, Ann too began to smile.

"Hi!" the man said, "I'm Rick. That was great the way you handled her! Somewhat of an airhead, wouldn't you say?" Smiling he held out his hand to shake.

"Oh, thanks! I'm Ann." she said taking his hand. "And, yes, definitely an airhead. I'm not so sure that she is unique to the crowd though. There seems to be quite a few here!"

Ann and Rick took off from there with a casual conversation. The typical "What do you do for a living?" and "Are you from here?" transpired in no particular order.

Phillip and Andrew decided to wander off and "mingle" with some of the other familiar faces, following direct instruction to stay close, where their mother could see them.

Moments later, Mike and Sharon, approached the boys. Sharon and Ann had been friends for ever it seemed. Sharon and Mike had been married for about a year after meeting in Michigan. Sharon's parents live in Detroit and, while Sharon was staying with her parents temporarily, she met Mike at a public gathering. Mike was the police commissioner at the time, but had since retired and moved to Arizona where he and Sharon married.

"Hey, guys!" Sharon hollered at them.

"How are you, Uncle Mike, Aunt Sharon?" Phillip asked with that same emotionless expression on his face. Phillip had not smiled or laughed for months now.

"What's going on guys? You okay? How are you both holding up?" Sharon asked.

"I guess we're doing alright, how are you guys?" Andrew asked.

"We're good. How's your mom? Where's your mom?" Mike asked

"She's right over there," Phillip answered, pointing at his mom, who was still talking to the same guy.

"Who's that she's talking to? New guy?" Sharon asked

"I don't know about that, but at least she's talking to someone." Came a voice from behind them. Turning around, they saw Jack who had, apparently, decided to avoid letting anyone in on his grand entrance.

"Jack!" Sharon shouted while hugging her long time friend, "How are you?" She asked stepping back from him.

"I'm good, Cher!" Jack replied, "How are you?"

"Wow!" Sharon replied, "Long time no talk to!"

"Hey, everyone, how is Ann holding up?" Jack addressed everyone at the table.

Phillip was the first to reply to his uncle Jack, "She got dressed for the first time today. She's usually in my dad's pajamas and hardly gets out of bed anymore."

"Well, then, I guess today is a good day!" Sharon said with that same amount of happiness in her voice.

The boys loved how happy Sharon always was. She always made the boys look at the brighter side of things. Once when Andrew was having a hard time with one of the other kids at school, it was Sharon who taught him how to handle that kid. He learned from Sharon how to approach this kid without making things worse and, it worked. Now, Andrew and Billy hung out together all the time.

"Come on!" Sharon looked at both of them. They knew it was more of an order than a request. "Walk over to the counter with us for some food. I'm starved! Mike, you must be famished!"

The boys diligently followed them to the buffet line.

They found a picnic-type bench to sit at when Mike and Sharon set their food down to begin talking to the boys.

Just then, James walked past. James was another very dear friend of the family whom none of them had seen in quite some time. Sharon, Mike and James all had spent time with Wayne and Ann in the past, so they all were good friends. As Sharon sat down, she looked at James, "Hey, guy! Long time!"

"Mike, Sharon, how are you?" James asked them.

"We're okay. How are you doing? We were just sitting down with the fellas. Ann is over there," Mike said pointing to Ann and the guy she was talking to. "We thought we would get caught up on how these two are holding up, if you know what I mean."

"Sure," James said. "I'm glad I ran into you guys. I was hoping maybe you would have some information on Wayne and what happened to him. The story I got seemed a bit out of the ordinary and I was hoping maybe you guys could help clear the air for me."

This, Mike knew was his 'golden opportunity' to get some things off his chest to someone who might be able to help relieve some of the burden he had been carrying around all this time.

"Listen, there's something we want to talk to you about, it might involve Wayne's accident." Philip and Andrew were both listening intently.

"Hey, fella's," Mike said. "Maybe you ought to find something else to do."

Phillip said, "Please, Uncle Mike. Don't leave me out of this. He was my dad!"

Mike gave into his 'little buddy' as usual. "Okay, kid. For a little while, I guess, but when I tell you to go, you go." Phil sat back down nodding in agreement. Sharon began the conversation.

"Mike and I can't help but think that there is something more to the story than Ann is aware of. Actually, I'm not sure I know anything at all about what I'm talking about, but I can't help but feel like the information I received is important. Mike, why don't you take the floor on this one?"

"What are you talking about?" James asked her.

"We haven't really heard from Ann since Wayne's death. I can't imagine what she is going through right now, but what I can tell you is that she and Wayne were the 'couple of the town' according to all who knew them. She was bright, always laughing and making others laugh as well. I can't believe that she will ever accept what happened to Wayne. I don't expect you to understand fully, boys," she said, looking at the kids, "but your parents loved like most people only dream possible, so it stands to reason that she would be very sad, making all attempts possible to find a reason for your dad's death."

Looking back at James, Mike took over the conversation.

"There are some things about Wayne that I never thought I would be talking to you about." Mike looked at James

"Like what?" James asked

"Okay, here it goes," Mike began hesitantly. "We all have known both Wayne and Ann for a very long time. You know that Wayne was from Michigan, right?"

"Yeah?" James said

"He moved here rather abruptly following the death of his first wife."

"Wayne mentioned something about that quite a while ago, although I don't have any of the details. All I know is that they weren't together for long and their marriage was having difficulty. Wasn't she killed in a car accident, or something?"James asked.

"That's the story anyway. There was never much of an investigation. Wayne had gone to the scene following the identification of his wife and discovered that there were two sets of tire tracks. One set went completely off the road, the other appeared to swerve and disappear as if the second vehicle skidded enough to leave marks in the ice and then regained control and continued on. There was only one vehicle reported in the wreck, but there was damage to the side of the car that wasn't mentioned in the report."

"Do you think she was forced off the road, Mike?" James asked. "If that's the case, why didn't you ever pursue this before?"

"It's actually very complicated and that was a long time ago. I didn't get much information at the time, since I wasn't involved in the investigation. It was kept pretty quiet; besides, there were other things going on at the time." James could tell that Mike was getting a bit defensive.

"So what about Wayne?" James asked. "What do you want to do about his death? I get the impression that you're here because you think this might be more than a hit and run. Am I right, Mike?"

"Okay, boys, go get your mom, would ya?" Mike said, wanting to open up the conversation without the boys around to hear him.

"Alright!" Andrew said. "We'll be right back. Come on, Phil."

The boys trotted off toward their mom.

"Wayne had an 'acquaintance' from Michigan that turned out to be not such a good one. They were together for only a brief period of time, but this gal told everyone that she and Wayne were madly in love. Actually, Wayne thought she only wanted to use him to help her raise her kid. He said she was a real psycho. Anyway, she lived with him for about six months. As a matter of fact, I think she was put in prison for a few years and just got out. No one knows what happened to her, but she was well known for holding resentment and getting back at people. It's possible that she had something to do with all of this because she was seen with one of the Bone Breakers in Michigan. I think they were dating."

"So, why do you think she might be involved with Wayne's death?" James asked him.

"Because Wayne was involved with the Bone Breakers back in Michigan. He took off, and I'm sure there was some unfinished business with them," Mike offered.

"What 'unfinished business'?" James asked. "And how do you know about all of this?"

"I have my connections. And I'm not sure what he left behind. Wayne was in an accident prior to his death. It appeared that he was run off the road, but he wouldn't go into much detail when asked. All I know is that he sustained some extensive injuries and was bed ridden for some time."

Just then, Ann walked up to the table with the man she had met. "Hey everyone! The boys said you wanted to talk to me. This is Nick. Nick," she said turning to him, "this is Sharon, Mike and James! Hey James!" Ann went over to James to hug him. Suddenly, she began to cry with her face buried in James' shoulder.

"Hey, kid!" he said, holding her. "It's gonna be okay. You're a tough young broad! Wayne believed in you and so do the boys. I'm back now, and I'm here if you need me, okay?"

"Ah, wow, Jimmy! I missed you!"

James was always around when Ann needed him. He was kind of like a best friend to her, more like a brother. They had become friends with a strange sort of connection when Wayne introduced them. Jimmy was involved in a class that Wayne attended when he first came to

Arizona. So he and Wayne had known each other longer than Ann knew either of them but still, the two of them hit it off. Because Jimmy knew Wayne so well, he and Ann would get together, usually to plot something evil and twisted for Wayne's birthday parties. They had a great deal of fun in doing so, especially for the last birthday Wayne had. It had something to do with a night out, an invitation for a hooker in a birthday cake, and Ann covered in frosting wearing only a teddy that Wayne bought for their anniversary.

This individual that Mike was talking about, Laurie, was just recently released from prison after serving four years of a six-year sentence for breaking and entering. The records state that she was picked up after being seen inside the senator's office one evening. Since her release a year ago, she has disappeared. No forwarding address, only that she was on probation and would be for about two more years.

"Well, I ask you this because apparently she and Wayne were involved with some of the same people back in Michigan at different times, but there may be a connection to her and your husband's death, Ann."

Mike and Sharon looked a bit anxious.

"Okay," Ann responded, "If what you say is true, then what am I supposed to do about it?"

They could hear the irritation in Ann's voice and, everyone understood why.

"Hey," Nick said to Ann, "Maybe I should go somewhere else and leave you all alone to talk about this."

"No," Ann said to him. "Let's you and I go for a walk around town. How's that sound?"

"You sure?" Nick asked.

"Yep. Come on. Sher, will you keep an eye on the fella's for me?"

"You got it, kiddo," Sharon said.

As the two of them walked away, Rick said to Ann, "Who is the individual they were talking about, this 'Laurie' person?"

Looking back at Rick, Ann said, "Wayne was a very talented welder and had built his own custom motorcycle. It was everything to him. Of course he was only about twenty years old at the time. Can you imagine building your very own motorcycle at such a young age? He didn't just build it, though; he actually *designed it!* Anyway, because Wayne had some issues with his driver's license, he trusted Laurie, his girlfriend at the time, to put the bike in her name so he could get it registered. She went completely psychotic on him when she found out he had no intentions of marrying her. He didn't love her or the rotten kid she was raising so she sold the bike on the front driveway and split with the money. Nice, huh?"

"I can understand why you don't like her!" Rick replied with a look of bewilderment.

"It gets worse. Laurie not only split with the money and, gratefully, her kid, but she also contacted the Arizona DMV to report him for his suspended license in Michigan to ensure he wouldn't get one here. The good news is that it backfired because I was able to investigate and get Michigan to release the suspension based on the seven-year statute of limitations on monetary gain, which is what the issue was about. His license was re-instated. Anyway, she was at the funeral, and she seems to be in the backdrops at the most inopportune times. I never really thought much of it other than being glad that I had him and she didn't. She had left him so abruptly, and he moved on. I suppose it's possible that she had a problem with that. She was a criminal, Rick. That much is true. When I looked her up, secretly, I found some charges on her that were pretty amazing. She was finally convicted for breaking and entering, but she's conveniently out and has been since Wayne's death."

"Forgive the intrusion, Ann, but do you hold yourself responsible in some way?" Rick asked.

"What are you some sort of psychologist?" Ann asked defensively.

"No, it's just that you gave the impression that you somehow feel guilty, that's all." Rick replied.

"I'm sorry, Rick." Ann said. "Yes, I suppose a part of me wishes I had never agreed to get Wayne that bike. Then again, he probably would have ridden the other one anyhow, so either way…" She wiped another tear from her cheek with the handkerchief Rick supplied her.

"This Laurie person had disappeared for a while since her release. There is no record of her location, meaning she has broken her parole. Whatever she's up to, it must be worth the risk of being on the run. Laurie was in pretty good with some real bad people in Michigan. People who didn't care much for Wayne."

"When was she released?" Rick asked.

"Two days before Wayne's death." Ann replied.

Mike and Sharon had brought up information from Mike's past when he was at the police department. Ann knew that Mike had some inside information regarding Wayne's past, but she had no idea what it was.

****

In 1964, a beautiful little boy was born to a couple that welcomed him as their fourth child to a family they considered to be perfectly content. They chose to name him Lucas and felt that with a personality such as the one he was developing, that he would be an asset to anyone whom might encounter him. He and his mother were very close, his father had a dry sense of humor that made people think twice.

Lucas was considerably younger than his siblings, so he spent much of his early years as that of an only child. As adults, his two brothers and one sister had become successful and very business oriented living in different states from their parents, but all in all, they maintained what they considered to be a strong family line.

Although he had never thought it possible when he was younger, Lucas had become the very proud father of the two most incredible boys in the whole world and husband to an amazing wife, whom he considered to be his soul mate. His boys were named Phillip and Andrew.

Phillip had grown to develop interests more like his father where Andrew was commonly found at his mother's hip.

Ann had noticed Andrews interest in her drawing and had discovered that not only did Andrew love to draw, but unbelievably he had developed his mothers talents. Ann's ability to draw portraits was something Wayne was not only secretly jealous of but found to be the most amazing talent he had ever seen. She made every portrait look as if the person's eyes in the drawing were following their admirer. Andrew was constantly caught lost in his drawing world right alongside his mother. Both Wayne and Ann knew that when Andrew was very young, that he was lost to the art world and that fishing and hunting, the "guy" things, were of little to no interest to him. That was interests left for Wayne and Phillip to share. Regardless, the four of them shared an enjoyable life together until that fateful day.

Ann was Wayne's absolute pride and joy and he was so proud of her. But he was feeling a bit of separation anxiety for his wife so he had called her that night. The boys were away with their schooling, leaving Wayne by himself in their big house, so Wayne had chosen to make plans with his lifelong friend, Jack.

Wayne and Jack had first met in Michigan when they were kids and as they grew up together had become inseparable. They had the same aspirations to become bikers and join a club. Probably a fairly silly ambition, although they didn't think so at the time, they hit it off immediately as kids and had been friends ever since. Jack was always looking to go do *something* on Friday evenings which generally meant drinking at a club. Be that as it may, Wayne never did anything without Ann's full approval and vice versa, especially when it involved drinking. He knew that the cop in her would kill him if he left their home after consuming any alcohol. She practically read him the riot act when he had a small glass of wine before running to the grocery store around the block. Incidentally, that particular afternoon, Wayne had walked.

When he decided to call her that afternoon, Ann suggested that he go out and find something to do. "Spend some time with your friends, honey, you're getting stir-crazy!" She said to him, "it'll help keep your mind off of things. I cannot imagine that I will be gone for too much longer. They're making the final repairs as we speak. I should be home by next week. When I get back, maybe we can go on a mini-vacation and get re-married. What do you think?"

"That sounds like fun, sweetie!" Wayne said to her, "you know we haven't done anything like that since the boys started school. We won't have to worry about sneaking out for a romantic dinner this time!" She knew full well that he was teasing her, even though part of him was serious.

Wayne took her advice and headed out to meet Jack. His intention was only to meet up with Jack and make plans from there. Then, a truck suddenly turned in front of him, giving Wayne no time to stop. In an instant, he was standing next to his motorcycle feeling no pain and wondering how that could be. Then, he saw two men jump out of the truck and start running away and even though he considered chasing them, they had already gotten too much of a head start, so he turned around to see if anyone was injured.

As he returned to the accident, a small group of people had gathered around in a semi-circle, so he moved closer to see what was going on and what everyone was looking at. Then, Wayne realized that the something was actually him, lying on the street, his right leg twisted in an odd way. Watching, Wayne stood helpless as the emergency personnel attached paddles to his torso and sending a current into his chest. They inserted a tube down his throat, monitors and an oxygen tank sitting beside him.

Wayne stood by to watch as his friend Jack stood next to some lady he had never seen before.

"Hey Jack!" Wayne shouted. Jack didn't look at him.

"Jack! Stop joking around! This isn't funny!" He tried to smack him in the shoulder as his hand passed through his body. Startled, he tried it again.

"I must be dreaming!" Wayne said aloud, but it appeared that no one could hear him. Jack and the lady walked over to a group of people.

"Did any of you see anything?" Jack asked them. The lady spoke up first.

"I did! I saw two men jump out of that truck!"

"I think you should be telling this to the cop, come on, I'll go with you!" Jack had said to the stranger.

Wayne is lying down again but cannot seem to open my eyes. Some men are now loading him onto a stretcher to be taken away with sirens blaring.

I hear shouting, "Give him another dose! Don't you die on us mister!"

Wayne can feel the vehicle come to a stop. Not really feeling anything other than air forced into his lungs by some sort of devise, he can only presume that he is being removed from the ambulance.

Now he sees his body taken into a large operating room with machines and stainless steel everywhere. Various individuals were scampering around the room shouting orders. More shouting from one of the men as he is standing next to Wayne's body.

"I need another dose over here now! Nurse! Call x-ray and get a chest STAT! You! Start the defibrillator!" Then another voice shouts, "Clear!" And another jolt of electricity surges through his body. "Almost! Keep going! We're losing him!"

"Nurse! Call in Cardiology and get me set up for an open, NOW!"

Wayne had joined Jack again and could see him talking to a police officer.

"Officer," Jack said, "all I know is that my friend was hit. I didn't get here until after the fact. This lady used Wayne's phone and dialed the first number that came up." Jack had his arm gently around the lady's shoulder. "That happened to be me."

"Yes sir!" the lady standing next to Jack said. "I saw that white pick-up truck with two men in it. They took off running that way!" She pointed to the other side of the street. "One was wearing a white T-shirt and blue-jeans; the other was wearing black or dark blue shorts and a green T-shirt. I think they were both either white or Mexican. Anyway, I am a nurse and I was more concerned with getting the young man breathing again. Do you know which hospital they will take him to?"

"Not yet, ma'am, but if you wait, I can find out for you." The officer then focused his attention on the detectives who were investigating the truck.

Then, the woman began eagerly telling a different officer that she noticed that one of the men, the one in the shorts, had a terrible limp and both of them had dark hair. No glasses, or other outstanding features that she could remember.

"I do remember one other thing" she said, "the one in the blue-jeans did have a mustache and a goatee. I am sorry officer. I cannot believe they just ran off like that after possibly killing that poor man!" She turned back to Jack to hand him a card.

"You're a friend of his?" she asked him

"Yes and thank you so much for your help. His name is Wayne and he is my best friend. His wife is away in Texas right now, so if you'll excuse me, I must make the worst phone call of my life."

"I understand, listen, here is my card. When you can, will you please call me or have his wife call me. I would like to help in any way that I can." Tears began falling down her cheek. Quickly, Jack hugged her. "Thank you!" Jack said and turned to call Ann.

Wayne arrived at the hospital only to be taken immediately into surgery. The personnel were unable to get his heart to continue beating and, following a chest x-ray, had discovered that he had extensive damage to the arteries. By the time he had arrived, he had suffered two heart attacks with complete cessation of the organ.

Having left her vehicle back in Texas, Ann was on an emergency flight back. Wayne is sitting next to her, unable to touch or speak to her.

"It's going to be okay, honey! I am right here with you!"

Ann arrived at the hospital to see Wayne's body lying on the bed. His right leg was completely mangled and his head and chest were swollen to the point of non-recognition. Despite the physical appearance, she rubs his arm and covered his hands to keep them warm. Bending over, she whispers softly to him.

"I love you baby, more than you will ever know! You promised me that we would grow old together and that we would even die on the same day and today is not that day! Please don't give up on us my love, I need you to come back to us, baby! Please!"

Years ago, when they had first met, Ann remembered a conversation that the two of them had. We had been dating by this time and had not been able to spend much time together. She remembered both of them spending so much of their lives together working instead of spending time together. Now, all she wanted was time back. She wanted the two of them to get away from their lives and spend time vacationing or something.

Looking at his body lying there in front of her, she was having a hard time being positive. She had seen many people never make it out once they were placed in this type of medical and physical state.

The swelling in his face and chest indicated to her that the outcome couldn't possibly be in their favor. She felt him respond as she leaned down to kiss him on the cheek.

"Mom?" Ann said turning to her mother who had just entered the room. "Did you see that? He turned his face to me when I kissed him."

With tears in her eyes, Alice hugged her daughter. "Yes, honey, I did see that."

Alice knew that there was no hope for Wayne to survive this time. She had seen this man survive many things over the years, but this one was not going to bring back her son-in-law. She couldn't tell her daughter this, though. This was her best friend that was laying on this bed. This was the man that she saw make her daughter's entire life a wealthy, rich, happy success and now all of that stood a strong chance of disappearing. How does a mother help her own daughter get through this?

She looked at Ann and said quietly to her, "Talk to him, honey. Keep talking to him."

"Its hopeless, isn't it Mom? He's never coming back to me, is he?"

"No, honey. It isn't hopeless. He never left you and he still hasn't. Wayne will always be a part of you, no matter what you do, where you go, or how you live. Even if he doesn't pull out of this, he will never leave you. Now, *talk* to him!"

Turning back to him, Ann bent down to her husband once again. I love you, baby! Go to sleep for me now and know that we will see you again one day. I will be okay, I will live for both of us. You go to sleep. I love you more than life itself and want you to be free from all of this. I love you." With that, Ann kissed him as the tears fell on his soft, cold, skin. She wrapped his hands one more time and asked for a warm blanket to cover him. To the nurse, Ann said,

"I don't ever want you to let him get cold. He hates to be cold, so I want him covered with warm blankets. Can you please do that for me?"

"Yes, ma'am, I will be right back." She turned to leave.

Again, Ann remembered a time a number of years ago when she and Wayne were still dating. She had just been to the doctor and had received some upsetting news. Over the past few weeks, she had been very ill. She wasn't able to keep any food down and had lost a great deal of weight.

The doctor had told her that he was going to rule out any serious diseases and she remembered how scared she was at the time. When she sat down to talk to Wayne about it, he had given her a look that she knew she would never forget. Funny how things like that are not important until one is placed in a position such as the one she found herself in now. She never dreamed of living her life without this man since she always knew that she would live the rest of her life with him.

In the end, the results did come back negative and they both shared an overwhelming feeling of relief. Ann remembered wondering how he would make it if anything ever happened to her. Suddenly, she was placed in a position of having to consider readjusting her life to one she wasn't familiar with. Her friend, Donna, and she had discussed how Donna was able to move on after losing her husband. They had sat together countless times reminiscing about him, then suddenly, she was alone.

It's hard to consider such things in life when they are taken for granted. Sitting in front of her husband, Ann looked at him and said, "Wayne, please forgive me for not appreciating every moment of our lives. I took so much for granted and now I realize what I am about to be faced with. I'm not sure I am strong enough to get through this. I don't know where I'm expected or supposed to start. How do I raise our boys alone? How do I keep our house, alone?" Crying, she knew that her life was expected to continue and that, somehow she would have to learn to get through this.

✳✳✳✳✳✳✳✳✳

I have learned that I am not allowed back into my body. The damage was much too extensive, and, looking at myself lying on the hospital bed, I'm not sure this is upsetting for me. As I watch my loving wife holding my body, continuing to caress my arm and hand, she knows that I am no longer there; she looks hurt, weak, and so very sad. Ann is the strongest woman I have ever known, seeing her like this has brought about a fear in me that I cannot describe. I know we had discussions in the past regarding this exact scenario; however, I never thought they would come true. She was right; we promised to be together forever, and I cannot rest until I know why that was taken away from us. I miss her very much, although I know we will be together one day. We are soul mates; I know that we will reach that destiny one day. The closeness that we shared was so impenetrable on earth that I am certain our souls will come together once she joins me. But she must come to me through natural causes, not by her own doing. My spirit cannot ascend until I am certain that she will live her life to the fullest as she did with me.

I am with her at the police station where she and our families are listening to the detective discuss the case.

"We are still investigating the accident, so I have no further details at this point. We ran the plates on the truck which, as I'm sure will come as no surprise to you, was stolen. Because this was a hit and run, we are giving this investigation top priority. Oh, one more thing, can any of you think of any reason why anyone would want to hurt Wayne?"

"Are you kidding me? Everyone loved that man!" my wife exclaims.

"I only ask," the detective interjects, "because the truck was registered in New York."

"New York?" Jack interrupts. "An awful long way from home, weren't they? Do you think this was intentional?"

"I have no reason to believe that this was not an accident, the individuals running merely out of fear. There are many reasons a person might run from such a horrific scene," the detective claims. "I would just like to know if there is any reason anyone can think of that might give us a lead other than a simple hit and run accident, it would be greatly appreciated."

Ann left the room, went to the restroom and vomited.

******

In 1962, a member of the American Mafioso revealed that, in America, the Mafiosi began to refer to their organization by the words Cosa Nostra. This is an organization consisting of groups called "families" or "clans" run similarly to that of a pyramid style, the structure begins with a "boss" aided by a second-in-command with one or more advisors. Other than its members, the Cosa Nostra utilizes "associates" that are individuals outside the family who function as aides or workers. It is these associates that the family members can assign to various tasks without creating any suspicion when necessary. Without considering all the intricate details of how the "family" functions, in all actuality, they are a hidden organization that most don't want to reckon with. Once an individual is involved with this group, there is no leaving them.

In Michigan, the Mafia was attempting to obtain control of the state by utilizing groups of associates to gather information. These selected groups had to be not only loyal but dependable as well.

In New York, the Cosa Nostra, the mob, was controlled and led by Guido Valente who had discovered a local biker organization that was well known to most who resided along the east coast as The Bone Breakers. This club was more than willing to work with Guido in order to help him establish power. The return would be the establishment of a club feared by everyone across the United States that held more power than any other.

It's well known that with power comes money and success. This was an interest to Savage, aka Sam, the originator of the Broken Bones. Sam had worked his entire adult life trying to obtain power across the country and, working as an associate for Guido and Frankie gave him that potential.

Although they had originated in New York, by the time Luke was a teenager, the club had broadened their establishment to Michigan where they had yet to establish full control.

After finishing high school, Luke decided to fulfill his own desires and become a very strong member of the Bone Breakers. Over time, he held a status so powerful that all members of both organizations had grown to fear him. The Bone Breakers, like the mob, were led by Frankie Sarducci who was Guido's nephew. This meant that the Bone Breakers were separate from the mafia but were still controlled by Frankie. While Guido ran his organization out of New York's busiest, most popular dance hall in lower Manhattan, Frankie was making all final decisions with their business transactions in Michigan.

The Cosa Nostra held a primary interest in state control with a focus on two main commodities, money and power. This desire meant developing any possible plan to control all illegal money transactions within the state regardless of the extent. It was Frankie's responsibility to obtain control of all drug dealings throughout Detroit making sure to receive a large percentage of every transaction. The reward to the dealers were that he offered full protection. His members were numerous enough to maintain a large business enterprise, and the benefits to his group certainly outweighed the repercussions.

Guido and Frankie both were greatly feared by most, as neither man had any remorse for taking a life. In fact, they had no problem taking the lives of families should either deem it necessary. Eventually, Guido had redirected much of his focus on acts of corruption in an effort to obtain power over the states, more specifically Michigan and New York, with the intention of eventually owning the entire East Coast.

These corruptive acts would generally focus on political figures by obtaining information that would jeopardize their reputation. The mob would go out of their way to gather whatever information they could to hold over a given individual's head. Should this information, somehow not be made available it was not unheard of for Guido to call on Lucas for help.

Because of the powerful status Luke held, it made no sense to Guido to place such an asset in harm's way. It was Luke who directed members of the club to go after whomever necessary and by any means necessary, even if that involved murder.

Because Luke was merely an associate, having him in charge of assigning individuals with lower status to carry out the job would protect the integrity of the mob bosses.

During his involvement, he was never charged with any crimes, only called to testify on behalf of the family.

During one such case, Luke was placed in a position where his testimony could have either revealed important facts disclosing information to the authorities, breaking apart the entire family and changes the political powers of the state or protect any associate involved with such accusations. At the time of his involvement, Luke never really gave the caliber of the crimes that were committed much thought. In all actuality, he was only responsible for the assignment and making sure his orders were carried out. Although he was never really placed in a position of actually murdering another human-being, the information he had gathered over the years made him not only valuable, but also an extreme threat. Voluntarily leaving the club was not an option for him.

Guido and Frankie had a very extensive family which was not unheard of with the mafia. Frankie's nephew and godson, Michael Santino was appointed police commissioner, giving him control over who was arrested. Rarely were any of their boys in either organization arrested since even the police officers were instructed to look the other way by Commissioner Santino.

After a couple of years of involvement with the club, Luke had found a woman that he quickly fell madly in love with. He had not known that it was possible to love so much that he might consider a different and safer lifestyle. But the money was plentiful enough that changing careers would mean that he would not be capable of providing Kay with everything in life she needed. He was living on top of the world with top of the line cars and a mansion that took anyone's breath away that was invited in to see it. Now, suddenly, Luke was considering giving all of this up for his new wife.

Kay was unaware of his full involvement with the club and knew nothing about his activities with the mob. Keeping his business life as far away from his home as possible, Luke was keeping secrets from this woman he wanted to be in his life, for the rest of his life. The responsibility of keeping Kay safe was left up to him, until she made a fatal mistake. One that Wayne would not be able to protect her from.

They were married less than a year when the worst thing imaginable had happened to her.

Kay had taken his hand in marriage and had promised to love and commit herself to him forever. They had their problems, but nothing that made him believe she was capable of doing what she did.

They had been having some difficulties with their marriage, including frequently arguing over financial issues. At the time, Luke thought these topics were common and that time would sort them out, until one evening when she came to him informing him that she had gotten herself into trouble.

"What is going on with you, Kay?" Luke asked her.

"Luke, I don't really know how to tell you this, and I don't expect you to understand, but I have been seeing another man." Tears welled up in her eyes.

"What? Kay, what are you saying?" Luke had asked her. "Why would you do something like that, Kay? Haven't I given you everything you need?" he had become very angry. Luke had already come to the realization that she was hiding something from him, but because of the frequent arguing, he felt it best to let her come to him instead of giving them something else to argue about. Growing tired of continually fighting with her he knew deep down that the relationship was quickly coming to an end unless something was done.

After telling him that she was having an affair, Kay had explained to him that she was now in fear of her life.

"Luke, I know you are angry and hurt, and I am so sorry. I am a stupid woman for thinking I could do something like this to you." she said with a look of fear on her face.

"What do you want from me, Kay? If you're looking for an approval for a divorce, then I suppose you will have to wait because I can't think straight right now. I wanted us to repair this relationship, not destroy it." Luke had given the impression that he was about to storm out of the room.

"Luke! I need your help. Please don't leave and listen to me I'm scared! The guy I became involved with is going to kill me if I stop seeing him!" She falls to the floor, sobbing.

"What do you mean?" Luke crouches down next to her desperately awaiting her explanation.

"I think he is a very dangerous man. I am so very sorry! Please, is there any way you can forgive me?" She continues to cry.

"We can deal with that later. What makes you think he is dangerous? Dangerous, how?"

"Well," she begins to explain, "When we first began seeing each other, he was pretty much always available when it seemed like you weren't, Luke. I was just feeling lonely and unimportant to you but you wouldn't talk to me."

She was right about that, Luke had been absorbing himself so much into the family, that he left Kay alone often.

"He made me feel like I was on top of the world until, all of a sudden, he became mean and demanding that I figure a way to spend time with him on his schedule. I couldn't do that, Luke. I never wanted us to divorce. I never meant for our lives to go this way. I don't know, I made a terrible decision and, maybe you can't forgive me for what I have done. Anyway, he started getting angry and would force me to do things that I didn't want to do."

"Okay," Wayne interrupted, "Why didn't you leave him back then if he was such an abusive person?"

Luke was not understanding why she or woman would allow a man to treat them that way. One thing he absolutely hated was a man who would beat his wife, or any woman for that matter.

He was under the impression that, although he was not home often, he had placed Kay on top of the world with all of the riches he provided her. It never occurred to him that she would go elsewhere for the compassion she needed and now she, his pride and joy, had been abused by another man.

"I told you, I was scared and by the time I actually learned how controlling he was, I guess I didn't know how to approach him. I'm so sorry, Luke, but you're the only one that can help me and now Tony is threatening you as well. When I told him I was finished with this treatment, he told me that he would kill me before he allowed me to stop seeing him and then he told me that he would get rid of you if he had to. Honey, I'm really scared that he is going to come after both of us!"

"Okay," Luke said to her, "so he knows who I am as well. How much did you tell him about me?"

"Only your first name."

"Does he know where you live?"

"I don't know. I never brought him into our bed, if that's what you're getting at. Will you protect me?" Kay was pleading with him.

"Of course I will, Kay, I will do anything in the world for you. But it is imperative that you tell me how much he knows about me."

"He knows what you do for a living and that you are a member of the Bone Breakers" she said.

"What I do for a living. What did you tell him?"

"That you're a welder. I never told him where you work, though."

"Okay, what is this guys name?" he asked her.

"Louie Santino" she told him.

A couple of days later, Frankie called Luke with a job to get rid of the two individuals assigned to obtain information on state senators. These guys had taken the information in question to the rival club to see if they could get more money for it than the Bone Breakers were willing to pay. Because they were bragging about how they planned to release the information to the highest bidder, one of Frankie's associates heard about their plan and reported it to Frankie.

"Who's the target?" Luke asked him.

"Louie Santino and Antonio Camboni" Frankie said. "You need to get rid of Antonio's wife and some girlfriend that Louie was seen with as well."

Luke knew it would be impossible to carry out this job. He wasn't sure who to assign to kill his wife, but the danger she was involved in was to such a degree that he wasn't sure how to go about doing this.

Knowing he had no choice, Luke contacted one of the associates that was new to the family, Sal. Luke informed him to create a car accident that would certainly result in a fatality.

"Take care of it immediately, Sal." Luke informed him. "I want it quick and as painless as possible."

Kay was driving on a back road that was not well maintained in the winter when Luke was informed of the accident. According to authorities, she had somehow lost control of her vehicle and slid off the side of the road, killing her instantly. The accident revealed that she was found with another person in the car, identified as Louie Santino.

Following Kay's death, Tony and Luke had staged our deaths to mislead the Cosa Nostra in order to get away from the danger they in.

Once Frankie found out that it was Wayne's wife that Louie was having the affair with, they would come after him as well. Tony would be considered guilty by association, so planning the demise of both of them seemed the only logical thing to do.

The year of Kay's death was an election year and two high powered candidates were running for State Senate in Michigan. Guido wanted information on both men that would force them to bend to the mob's wishes. Knowing that one highly probable candidate was involved in illegal sexual conduct Guido wanted to utilize control by collecting as much incriminating evidence as he could. This way, he could control the state through politicians by holding this information over their heads. The two individuals from the mob assigned to evidence gathering were Louie Santino brother of Michael Santino and Antonio Camboni. Louie and Antonio gathered the information and pictures as instructed – proof that the one candidate was having sexual relations with minor children while the other had a serious cocaine and prostitution habit. Obviously, because of the incriminating potential, the evidence they gathered could be sold for a substantial sum which our rival club had offered to double. But Louie and Antonio had hatched their own scheme to collect money from both clubs.

To complicate matters even further, prior to her death, Kay had disclosed to Luke that she had stolen some items from Louie in the hopes that it would somehow offer them both protection from Louie.

Showing them to Luke, Kay had no idea of the caliber of the situation she had placed them both in.

"Kay! You fool! Do you know who this is in these pictures? My God! You need to get these back to Louie! These pictures are of a senator and they need to be returned. Kay, they will kill you for these pictures!"

"How so you propose that I do this?" Kay inquired of me. "Should I just go up to him and say, 'Uh, just kidding Louie! Ha! Ha! You can have these back now!' For God sakes, Luke!"

"Okay", I reply to her, "but *why* would you steal something like this from him?"

"Actually, I have no clue. I guess I just thought that it might be a way to protect us from any harm if I had something of value, ya know?"

So, now Luke had the evidence that the entire New York mafia would be looking for in his possession. It was possible that no one would be able to connect him to these photographs and that they might come in handy in the future, so he chose to preserve them as best he could by locking them into his private safe. Luke had to assume that Kay had placed both of them in great danger.

The family would go after anyone with even a remote acquaintance to the person they were looking for. Knowing that, Luke had to be prepared for any possible retaliation.

Two days later Louie's body was found in the car with Kay when she was run off the road. Because of the politics involved, it came as no surprise that the authorities bypassed any in-depth investigation and reported Kay's death as an accident. After he received the news, Luke immediately packed the necessary belongings with the intention of getting out of Michigan as fast as possible. After changing identities to Wayne and Jack, and successfully faking their own deaths by staging an accidental explosion at a warehouse where they both worked, they left Michigan as fast as possible. Wayne's family was left with the impression that their youngest child was dead. Luke knew that he would eventually be able to inform his parents of his new location once the heat died down and Luke was sure they were not watching his family.

To date, Senator's Friese and McKnight were still in office meaning that the Cosa Nostra and the Bone Breakers had not taken control of the state. Because of this, both the mafia and the Bone Breakers would be after Wayne and his family if they knew that he was still alive and had the information they were looking for. There was only one person other than Wayne and Jack that could have leaked his existance to anyone in Michigan and that would be Laurie.

Laurie and Wayne had met shortly after his arrival to his new life. He was attending a rehabilitation class because he had decided to rid himself of the drug and alcohol addiction he developed while in Michigan. When they first met, she came across as a sincere, open hearted individual. Shortly after they began dating on a regular basis, they made the decision to live together. Laurie had a little boy from a previous relationship whom Wayne was not very fond of, but learned to tolerate with great difficulty. But the issues involved with Laurie as a single parent at such a young age created a severe amount of animosity between them.

Jack and Wayne had put together their first motorcycle from scratch. Wayne drew up the plans and Jack helped him weld the frame design, a creation that made this motorcycle not only unique but also worth more money than anyone could possibly imagine. After about seven months of being together, Wayne returned home from work to find most of our personal items missing including his motorcycle. It wasn't until later that one of the neighbors informed him that she was seen her accepting something from some man, possibly money, who had then loaded Wayne's motorcycle onto his truck.

Having found a note, Wayne knew that she had been working on her deceitful plan for quite some time. His motorcycle and his girlfriend were both gone in only one day. Although he knew that their relationship was doomed from the beginning, he never dreamed that she would actually sell his property and run with the money. He never did find out how much money she had sold the motorcycle for.

Neither of his parents had inquired as to why Wayne faked his own death; they only complied with his wishes of acting it through. This meant that neither of them had any information and Wayne could only pray that the mafia was not after them as well. Someone else was involved with Wayne's murder, someone who had informed Frankie or Guido that they were still alive. The only person that fit this description was Laurie. Laurie had come to Arizona from Michigan at the same time as Wayne's parents. This meant that she was most likely the person who had informed the Bone Breakers or the mafia of Wayne's whereabouts. If this was true Ann's life was in danger.

******

Ann has returned with a group of friends from her weekend out. Jack was there with her as was Cosmos who had followed them from the party. He is inebriated from alcohol and Ann and Jack knew he would be in need of sleep fairly soon judging by his actions. He was becoming belligerent and beginning to irritate them both.

"So," Bill asked "Cosmos, is it?"

"Yes." The man responded

"What do you want?" Bill asked. "Do you know Ann from somewhere?"

"No," he replied "I just met her today."

"Well, I have known her for a number of years. I'm sorry, why are you here?" Jack asked as Ann walked out onto the patio to join them. She had been inside gathering additional refreshments. As she handed a bottle to Jack, she realized that the conversation was becoming heated.

"I'm here, *Jack,* is it? I'm here because your *girlfriend* allowed everyone to follow her here. I can leave." He stood up and began to teeter sideways. Sitting back down, he let out a rude, disgusting belch.

"You're not going anywhere," Ann said to him. Looking at Jack, she set down her refreshment. They each got on either side of Cosmos and helped him into the house to lay him down on the couch.

"Ann," Jack said, "Do you know this guy?"

"I've never seen him before today, Jack, why?"

"He just seems familiar to me. I can't place him though. Are you sure you've never met him before? Maybe Wayne knew him?"

"No. Jack, are you kidding? This guy would have never gotten any of Wayne's time. He must be one of the most irritating individuals I have ever met!"

Cosmos' personality demonstrated that he was both ignorant in his views and very prejudice, something Ann had very little time for. This, in addition to his conversation created an unsettling feeling with both of them.

"Alright, Ann, what are you going to do now?" Bill asked her, "You and the boys can't have him here alone with you. Tell you what. I will stay in the spare bed room, he makes me nervous, Ann."

"Oh, Jack" Ann said, "That's so nice of you. But you do know what I do for a living, right? The boys are in their room right next to me, and I do have a gun, believe it or not! You go on home, I'll call you in the morning. Things will be just fine, don't worry!" Smiling, she showed Jack to the door.

"Okay, sweetie, call me tomorrow." Jack left

As Jack was driving home, it came to him who the man was. "Cosmos! Cosmos Sarducci! Now I remember who he is! Cosmos is one of the associates that Frankie and Guido hired in Michigan. He is a long way from home," Jack thought to himself. Turning his vehicle around, he headed back to Ann's house while calling her.

"Ann" Jack said when she answered the phone, "I'm coming back. Wait outside for me, I'll be there in a minute."

"Jack, what is it?" Ann asked him but he had already hung up the phone.

Jack arrived back at the house. Walking in, he motioned for Ann to follow him outside.

"Ann," Jack told her. "I remember why this guy looked so familiar to me. Wayne and I knew him from Michigan."

"Okay, that's a good thing," Ann was looking at him with a look of confusion, "So why did you come back?"

"I'm not going to get too into detail right now, but I do know that this guy is very dangerous. We need to get him out of here, Ann. He can't stay here."

"What are you talking about, Jack? Where are we going to send him. He can't drive in his present condition."

"I know, look, sit down and I will tell you as much as I know."

Jack began to tell Ann Cosmos' interest in both Wayne and Jack in their past.

"I don't think he recognized me, though. I would really like to keep it that way."

"Were you guys in some sort of trouble, Jack?" Ann asked him.

"No, it isn't that, Ann. We met him in Michigan through a mutual friend. There wasn't a great deal of involvement with him, which explains why he wouldn't have recognized me. Look Ann, just trust me on this one. The guy has a very tainted past and I don't want you or the boys left alone with him. I will stay here and make sure nothing happens, besides, I don't sleep very well anyway."

Ann let Jack stay in the guest bedroom. After locking the boys' door and her own, Ann went into her bedroom to retire.

Around 3 am, Ann awoke suddenly from sleep. Looking at the clock, she sat up to get herself a drink of water, when she saw Cosmos at the doorway of her room.

"How did you get in here?" Ann shouted.

"I opened the door and helped myself." He said

"Well, get out!" Ann screamed.

Jack ran up behind him, grabbed him and started shoving him toward the door.

"Do yourself a favor, Cosmos. Don't ever come around this house again!" Jack shouted as he threw Cosmos out onto the front walkway.

"You just made a big mistake, buddy!" Cosmos shouted as Jack slammed the door in his face.

Turning to Ann, Jack said, "I'm going to make sure that he leaves while you get yourself some sleep. We'll talk in the morning."

The following morning, Jack and Ann sat together for coffee when she broke the silence by asking him what had happened last night.

"Okay, here it goes. Ann, how much did you know about Wayne's past in Michigan?"

"Not very much, Jack, why?"

"Wayne and I both were members of a club called the Bone Breakers. This club is the biggest in the state of Michigan and New York. They have affiliates that are very powerful people to this day. Anyway, Wayne was one of the more important members and, Cosmos was an associate that took care of various situations that we all had brought to our attention. As you know, it takes a dangerous person to live their lives as criminals and that is exactly what Cosmos is. He will stop at nothing to accomplish a job for these people. I don't know for sure, but I believe that Cosmos is here to confirm that the individuals I speak of maintain that protection. In other words, I think he is here to take care of you, Ann."

"You mean you think he wants to *kill* me?" Ann asked

"Yes, I do. Why else would he have been trying to get into your room last night?"

"Well, I thought I locked the door. Apparently I didn't check it well enough, so that is my fault. But if he wanted to kill me, why didn't he just do it last night? Why would he wait?" Ann wondered

"You woke up and likely startled him." Jack responded, "don't underestimate him, Ann. Now he knows where you live and that you are the person he is looking for. We were talking about Wayne last night you know."

"So, now what?" Ann asked him, "you're telling me that my children are in danger, right?"

"Yes, Ann, I'm afraid so. Let me have them over to my house for a while until we can figure something out. That way, at least we can protect them immediately. Are you going back to work anytime soon?"

"No, but I can contact my friend Chris and fill him in on our concerns if you think that would be a good idea." Ann's friend Chris had been working at the police department since before she and Wayne had met. He was a wonderful friend of both of theirs, so she knew that he would have some advice for her.

"I'm not so sure that's a good idea just yet. Let me make a few phone calls and I will get back to you within the hour, okay?" Jack asked her.

Later that day, Ann was out riding around town when she decided to stop at a local coffee house. She had been sitting at the same table that she and Wayne had frequented on Sunday mornings. As she was reminiscing about some of the conversations they had shared, Ann found herself feeling empty and alone. She was trying so hard to get herself past the loss of Wayne and, after three months now of being without him, she was beginning to miss him more and more yet the probability of being able to live without him was feeling less and less likely.

Shaking her head in disgust, Ann got up to leave thinking that she would spend the day alone, riding around town. As she was leaving, Jack and a few of their friends pulled up outside.

"Jack!" Ann exclaimed in surprise. Walking up to give him a hug, she said, "What are you doing here?"

"Just looking for you, you doin ok?"

"Oh yeah," she said as she was wiping her face, "I was getting ready to go riding by myself, what are you doing?"

"Riding with you if you'll have us" Jack said.

"Sure, Jack," The tears started rolling down her cheeks again.

"Hey kid," Jack said pulling her back to him, "What's up? That Cosmos thing getting to you?"

Smiling she pulled back from him, "No. It's just that I think it's really starting to hit me, Jack. I was always the tough one in my family, but I'm not sure I will make it anymore."

"Hey, Ann" Jack said, "You're doing a fabulous job. Things are going to be tough for a long time, but you have everything in the world left to live for. Those boys need you to stay strong and carry on for their dad. Don't you *ever* think for a second that you can't survive this. Wayne let go because he knew you would be fine, I think you already know that sweetie."

Jack, Ann and the rest of their group prepared to leave. Ann was in the lead and as she pulled out into the intersection, a car bolted out of a parking lot and forced her off the road, sending her into a ravine. She and the motorcycle have traded places as it fell on top of her landing on her chest. Miraculously, she was only injured. Jack stayed at her side while they awaited the arrival of the ambulance.

The police arrived and, after the re-appearance of Cosmos, Jack knew that this was definitely planned as he informed the police of the accident. Following the report, they all left the scene to be with Ann at the hospital.

Cosmos and Sal are frantically driving away as Cosmos, in the passenger seat watchws behind making sure they were not being followed.

Turning to Sal, Cosmos said "Lucas' death was much easier than this one, Sal! Frankie is going to be pissed!"

"Oh, to hell with Frankie, Cosmos! What are we gonna do, go back and try it again?"

"All right, shut-up and just think of something!"

Jack knew that they were going to go after her again and next time, Ann might not be so lucky.

✳✳✳✳✳✳✳✳✳✳

Frequently, Ann found herself sitting alone in her drawing room thinking about Wayne. She had not produced any drawings in sometime; something that was unusual for her as drawing had always been the only activity that brought her any form of peace. One evening while sitting alone in front of a blank drawing page, she felt a warm presence next to her.

"Wayne," she says "is that you?"

She feels a sensation carry over her that sends goose pimples up her arms. There is a part of her that wants so desperately to believe that Wayne's spirit is with her, but logically, she feels that she is being ridiculous. Regardless, she begins to speak out loud, "Wayne, if that is you, *please* don't leave me. I need your help, Wayne. Bad things are beginning to happen and I don't know what to do." Ann begins to cry.

Straightening up, Ann wipes her face, shakes her head and mumbles aloud.

"Straighten up Ann. You're being ridiculous!" She says to herself.

Ann had previously promised Jack that she would attend a biker gathering with him following his relentless persistence. Accompanied by Jack and the boys, they all head out.

Once they arrive, Ann begins to mingle with people she has never met. She quickly discovered that it is more difficult to talk with people she already knew and that also knew or knew about Wayne. Not wanting to absorb herself back into the depression, Ann begins talking to a man that was standing by himself who offers her some kind words that seem to lift her spirits.

"Hello," he begins, "my name is Nick" he holds his hand out to her and she takes it.

"Nice to meet you," she replies, "I'm Ann."

"Are you here with someone?" he asks.

"I came up here with my friend Jack and my two boys. See? They're right over there. I guess they got bored either that or their stomachs are calling them." she says sarcastically.

They continue to talk, sipping on their own drinks and sharing stories of their riding experiences together.

"May I ask you something?" he asks her.

"Sure."

"Where is your husband? I see you wearing a wedding ring. Did he ride up with you?"

She begins to cry.

"Oh boy." he says, apologetically. "I didn't mean to upset you."

"No, it's okay. It's just that this is all so new to me still. He was recently killed, there was no way for you to know. I guess that it is still so fresh in my mind that I can't seem to control my emotions. I don't mean to make you feel bad. Please forgive me!" She attempts to wipe up her tears as he offers her a fresh handkerchief.

"Would you like to go for a walk and talk, maybe? We can window shop, and no one else will be the wiser." He gives her a hesitant smile.

"You know, that would be nice, but I want to let Jack and the boys know first."

They approach her kids, and are invited into a conversation about Wayne with the rest of the table. Ann avoids the conversation by letting them know that she is going to be walking up the street to window shop. She assures all of them that she will be fine and return within the hour.

"Boys," she says to Phillip and Andrew, "Will you guys be okay or do you want to go with me?"

"I'll go!" Andrew says, "Me too!" Phillip exclaims.

Turning to Rick, "Is that okay with you?"

"Of course," Rick replies, "Hey guys," he says to the boys, "There's a pretty neat shop up the road that I think you will like." He turns to Ann. "It's an antique store that carries a lot of old kids toys. Old metal trucks, things like that."

"Great!" Ann replies, "that should keep them busy!"

As they are walking, she offers him information on what happened to Wayne. "The truck that hit him was disabled from the blow and the drivers ran. Some lady gave a physical description of them, although I have heard nothing of the outcome so far. I can only assume that the two men got away."

"I won't tell you how, but I do have some connections and might be able to help you out a bit," Rick offers.

"Maybe," Ann replies as they head out for their walk

Ann wanted to let someone know of her concerns, yet wasn't about to share too much information with this particular individual since she had just met him. All she knew at this point was that Wayne had moved here from Michigan a number of years ago. He rarely talked about his past to her and whenever she asked him questions, he would change the subject. She knew he never lied to her, but now that she thought about it, she couldn't help but feel like she was missing something. At this point, she wasn't sure if she might be showing signs of diagnosable paranoia or something worse, maybe she was creating reasons to build a case on something that didn't exist. It was very possible and even probable that the individual's that hit Wayne ran because they were scared. Possibly that they *had* stolen the truck that hit him in from New York and ran now that they were guilty of now two severe crimes. Even after the past chain of events, Ann found herself wanting to avoid the belief that Wayne was actually murdered. Somehow, she thought that if his death was an accident, she would be able to deal with it better than if his death was a direct intent.

When Ann was speaking to the detective regarding Wayne's death, he asked her if she had any reason to believe that someone might want to hurt Wayne and couldn't get that conversation out of her head. She did know that he was involved with a "club" in his home state and that he had gotten himself into some sort of trouble, but because he never discussed this with her, she felt it best to let it go feeling that he was only trying to protect her, she just didn't know from what.

After they had walked around for a bit, Rick began to revert back to their conversation regarding Wayne.

"Look, Ann," Rick began, "I know you have no reason to believe me when I tell you that I might be able to help you, but if you would please let me do some checking from my end, then maybe I can find something that you might be overlooking. But if you do, you will have to give me more information." Because of her job, she would have to be very careful as far as what information she discussed and the questions she asked within the department. Besides, if there was club involvement believed, an outsider might be able to get information that the department may not have access or knowledge of.

"I suppose you're probably right, Rick," Ann was telling him, "let me think about it. If you have a card, I can give you a call and possibly we can talk further. You have to understand, I am a bit reluctant now that I am alone. My trust in other people just isn't there yet. Probably, this doesn't make any sense to you, and if you don't understand, than I am sorry."

"I do understand, believe me. Give it as much time as you need. I'm not going anywhere, and if you want me to do some checking, I will. I do have some limitation, but maybe I can get some information on the case from my connections. Did Wayne tell you the name of the club he was involved in?"

"It was the Bone Breakers." Ann replied.

A very reputable club, Rick knew all too well who these people were. He had lived in New York for 20 years. Coincidentally, Nick was born and raised in Manhattan and was actually a member of the Bone Breakers until he opted to move to the other side of the United States. He moved with a solid and positive relationship with the leader of the chapter and was, technically, considered to be a continual and committed member of the club even though he was living this far away. He figured it might be better to hold off on telling this lady about his exact involvement until the time was right, if it ever was. Being involved in such a large and reputable club had its benefits, and if her husband was killed because of it, probably he could get her some answers. He wasn't sure as of yet why he was so willing to help her out, or to even get involved. But there was something about her, something that drove him to wanting to help in whatever way he could.

"I'll give you my card, and you can contact me on Monday evening." He handed her a business card. "Now, promise me one thing, let's do some window shopping to get your mind off of this since there is nothing we can do at the moment, ok?"

"Okay," she says with a slight smile, "hey guys! Let's get headed up the road and see what else this town has to offer."

They begin walking when Rick says to her, "So tell me about your husband. What did he do?"

"Oh my gosh, everything. He was a welder, officially, but could literally fix and repair anything in our house. I have a studio in my home that he put together for me. He was so funny. Instead of buying the equipment I needed for my drawing and painting, he would insist on building it for me. He made me very proud to be his wife." she began to feel a lump developing in her throat.

Rick placed a hand gently on her arm, "It's okay to cry about it, Ann. You seem to be doing a tremendous job at holding yourself together and, although this may be somewhat uncomfortable for you, I won't tell a sole if I see you break down!"

She knew he was teasing by the look on his face.

"Thank you, Rick. I do appreciate that."

They continued to walk up and down the main street of the town until Jack caught up with them.

"Hey lady!" Jack hollers to her. "I thought you weren't going to be more than an hour!" He was smiling as he ran up to both of them.

Startled, Ann looks at her watch. "Oh great!" She exclaims. "I am so sorry Jack! I guess I lost track of time!"

"Mom!" Andrew jumps in front of her, "Look at the cool headband I found! Phillip bought it for me."

"Nice, honey!" Ann says looking at the headband Andrew was wearing. One of the things Andrew did with his father was share the attraction with motorcycle insignia on any piece of clothing, especially if his dad thought it was cool. Now his brother had bought him something that made Andrew beam with delight, something Ann hadn't seen in what seemed like forever.

"You're dad would love that on you, sweetheart!" turning to Phillip she put her arm around his shoulder, "thank you, honey. That was a very special thing you just did." Bending down to whisper to him, she said, "I'll slip you the money back later."

"No, Mom, that's okay. I have been saving it for Andrew's birthday anyway. I guess it's just early that's all." Smiling, Phillip said to his brother, "Okay, Andrew?"

"Okay, thanks!" Andrew went trotting off ahead to stick his nose up to another store window.

"Come on, kiddo!" Ann shouted to him, "Let's go home."

"What did you get, Phil?" Ann asked.

"Oh, just a crummy ol' model and this crappy knife!" Phillip replied with a grin on his face. "Aren't they awesome, mom?" He, too, had a large grin on his face.

"Yes, honey, VERY awesome!"

Smiling, Ann turns to Rick. "Well, I better head back. Thank you so much for the talk, Rick." She leaves him and heads back to her bike.

"Call me Monday!" Rick shouts back to her.

She waves as she runs off to her friends.

Ann has become very depressed since Wayne's death. Going out and meeting Rick was creating a sense of guilt in her, but the logical part of her knew that there was nothing wrong with moving forward with her life.

It was possible that Rick could help her with reaching some sort of closure because of his knowledge that he claims to have, but she was finding it difficult to believe him. If what he says was true, than he would know the power and intimidation of the clubs, something Ann only knew from a police perspective.

Ann was getting closer to believing that something was going on with Wayne's past and the more she thought about the Cosmos incident and the accident, the more she came to realize that her suspicions were justified.

What Ann didn't know was that Wayne had placed all activities with The Bone Breakers as well as the mob behind him when Kay, his first wife, died and never felt it necessary to share this information with Ann. Now that his past was catching up with her, she knew that taking action to protect herself and the boys was eminent.

✲✲✲✲✲✲

Ann was home working on a drawing she had started when the phone rang. She was trying to find some sort of inspiration and had decided to draw a portrait of her late husband, something she failed to do while he was alive.

Alive. Wow, she thought, that is not even normal to say. "When Wayne was alive" is something she could not see herself growing accustom to any time soon. He wasn't supposed to be dead and she knew it. Ann was trying to keep herself busy by doing basic chores around the house.

"Hello?" Her voice sounds shaky.

"Are you alone tonight?" It was Rick on the other end.

"Yes, why?" she asks, hesitantly.

"Would it be ok with you if I came by to talk with you? I found something you may be interested in, since I'm not too far away from your house, I thought maybe I could stop by and talk to you, this shouldn't take long."

"Actually, I would like that very much. I could certainly use the company. I'll put on a pot of coffee. Thank you!"

They both gathered on the back patio when he began to inquire about Wayne's past in Michigan.

"Exactly when did your husband move here?" He asks.

"About twenty years ago, following the death of his first wife."

"Did he tell you how she died?" He wondered.

"It was a car accident. Apparently, she careened off the side of the road one day during the winter months. The police told my husband that she lost control due to the black ice on the roadway. When he told me the story, he didn't really want to talk about it, so we just left the subject alone. Actually, I did try to look the case up, but never found anything. I guess that, at the time, I didn't really think much about it. Like I said, he never wanted to talk about his past, so I just dropped it. I'm not much of a believer in doubting the man I wanted to spend my life with, so I figured that, if there was something to her death, he would talk about it. He never did."

"Did his wife know anything about his involvement with any clubs?"

"Not that I know of. Then again, even I didn't know that much about his involvement. Why do you ask?"

"Was Kay from Michigan?" He does not answer her question.

"Yes, at least I believe she was. Like I said, I didn't get into searching his past, Rick. I trusted him to no end, not that I should have. Rick, why are you bringing this up now? All of this took place a long time ago! Jesus!"

"I understand that, Ann. But it is possible that your husband was involved with the Cosa Nostra. Do you know who that is?"

"Sure" she replies, "The Cosa Nostra is Italian for mob or mafia. Good god, Rick! Are you serious?"

"Maybe." He replied. Suddenly, she feels that she has been placed on the defense.

"Are you going to give me an explanation?" She inquires.

"Let me get some more information first, ok?" He gives her a look that makes her a bit uncomfortable. "You said that you shouldn't have trusted him. Why is that?"

"Can I tell you something?" she asked him.

"Sure. I know you haven't known me for long, but anything we discuss will be between us and I will only use it to help you, Ann, not to hurt you, okay?"

"I found out from a mutual friend that Wayne was involved in some pretty serious stuff with the club. Then, this guy came into my house that Jack had known from Michigan. In the middle of the night, I found him at my bedroom doorway while I was sleeping." She told him.

"Why was he in your home while you were sleeping?" Rick asked her.

"Because I made him stay. He was seriously intoxicated and I wasn't about to let him leave my home, is that okay with you?"

"Oh, wow, Ann. I'm sorry."

"That's okay, Rick. Jack stayed in my spare room to protect me as well. As soon as he woke up to my yelling at Cosmos, Jack kicked him out and I haven't seen or heard from him since."

"Cosmos? Is that his name?" Rick asked her

"That's what he told me. Jack knows him from Michigan and said that he was not a good person. She said that he was involved in some pretty dangerous stuff, but he didn't elaborate. I know that I should have dug deeper when I was talking to Jack, but I didn't think to do so at the time. Jesus, Rick, I can't even function as a cop anymore. The old me would never have acted this way, I'm not used to bringing both lives together, you know?"

"What do you mean by that?" Rick wanted to know.

"Only that, as a cop, I have always been able to separate work from my home life. Now, I cannot even protect my own children and myself. I just put myself into a life threatening situation, something I have *never* done before!"

"Well, I can't tell you how you are supposed to be as a cop, since I have never been one in the past. But I do have a story that I would like to share with you, something that happened to me not too long ago. I think it might help you."

"Okay, thank you, Rick. I'm listening." Ann said.

"I was involved in an accident a number of years ago. This accident left many people dead; it was a horrible pile up on the highway. Anyway, I had clinically died temporarily, obviously. When this happened, I saw the accident from above as if I was suddenly flying over from above."

Ann was looking at him with a look that must have suggested she wasn't believing him.

"Know this, Ann. I am not a religious person, and I don't know that I believe that there is a God, but what I saw was those people's spirits almost floating above their bodies."

"I'm sorry, Rick, this is not something I believe in." Ann said to him.

"Just hear me out for a minute, okay?"

Acknowledging that she would, Rick continued.

"The reason I tell you about this, is because I want you to know that Wayne is with you, his spirit is with you and always will be. You're never going to forget him, Ann, and he will never be without you."

"That was nice, Rick. Thank you very much for that story."

"I hope it helps you, Ann. I really do. I believe that the sole never really goes away, but that they stay with us as long as we let them."

Ann knew that Rick was only trying to make her feel better.

"Look," Rick said, "I have never told another person that story. All I'm trying to do is assure you that Wayne will never truly leave you. As long as you hold on to him and remember him, he will always be with you. Fight for what you believe in and don't ever give up, okay?"

"Rick, thank you so much for that!" Ann said sincerely, "That was a beautiful story and I appreciate you're intent. Let me ponder it for a moment, but thank you."

Rick left Ann's house until the following evening. When he returned, he had information regarding Wayne's first wife's death.

"I did some investigating into Kay's death and found no information with the name you provided me. Not having her maiden name, I can't seem to find her accident. Is there any place your husband may have kept some records of her? A safe deposit box maybe?"

"I don't think so" she thought for a moment, "Wait a minute! He does have a safe with some paper work in it. I haven't been able to go through it yet. We can check there if you want." Ann had not gotten to the point, yet, where she was able to go through Wayne's personal effects. Not only that, but she had not seen the inside of his safe in years and realized that she couldn't even recall what was in it.

"Well, I don't want to pry. If you are ok with me being here while you go through it that would be fine. Otherwise, you can contact me if you find anything." he said, with some obvious discomfort.

"Look, Wayne had no secrets from me. I can't imagine that we will find anything out of the ordinary. I have no problem with you being here. I'm sure we won't find anything that I don't already know about." She leads him to the office where the safe is located.

Opening the door of the safe and begins pulling out its contents. Inside, they discover an oversized envelope that Ann couldn't recall ever seeing before.

"Hey Rick. Take a look at this." She hands him the envelope. "I don't remember Wayne ever showing me this before. My God! I can't believe that in all these years, I have never seen any of the contents of this thing!" She reaches in and pulls out a piece of jewelry.

"What's that?" Rick asks.

"It must be Kay's wedding ring. I thought he buried it with her!" All of a sudden, she begins to cry.

"What is it?" Rick is standing next to her unsure as to whether or not he should continue to talk about this.

She looks at him with a smile on her face. "This is a blast from our past. It's been so long ago that I had forgotten all about it! Wayne bought this ring for me when we were first engaged. Because I am such a klutz, I had broken a few of the prongs off around the diamond in the center, see?" She hands it to him for him to inspect. "Anyway, we didn't have the money to get it fixed and the warranty expired. When he got the new promotion, he surprised me with this new full set wedding and engagement ring for our 2nd anniversary. We never did get this other ring fixed." She is staring at the ring remembering so many years ago.

"Maybe you should do that now." He suggested.

"Yeah, thanks, by the way, see what's inside this envelope. I don't remember ever seeing it before." She holds a manila envelope out to him.

Rick takes the envelope from her hand, sits down at the desk and begins to go through its contents.

"Do you mind if I hang on to this? I would like to look through it and see if I can find any more information from the names in here, if that's ok with you."

"Sure." Ann replies. "I don't have any idea what's in it, so I can't imagine that I might miss it. Maybe it'll somehow help."

Rick heads toward the door. "I'm going to take off now. Are you going to be ok?"

"Oh yeah." She replies. "I have to be!"

She follows him out to his car.

"Come over here a minute." He turns toward her and embraces her. Giving her a quick kiss on the cheek, he holds her for a moment in a hug.

"That's nice." She says. "Thank you."

Another quick kiss and he releases her while turning toward his vehicle.

"I'll call you tomorrow and let you know if I found anything. Do you have plans tomorrow evening?"

"Not at the moment." She replies.

"If you can keep your schedule open then how about I come by around 7 tomorrow night and we can go over any information I may have discovered. It's on my way home anyway. Besides, I kind of enjoy checking in on you. How are the boys?"

"They're doing good, considering. I am somewhat worried about Phillip. He doesn't seem to be coming out of the depression from losing his dad yet. They were so close. I'm not sure that I can help him out."

"Well, maybe we can all go fishing together. Maybe doing something like that would help him out?" Rick was trying so hard to be helpful, she knew.

"Yeah, we'll see. Thank you, Rick. I do appreciate the offer. At any rate, I will see you tomorrow night."

Waving good-bye, Ann headed into the house for the evening.

✳✳✳✳✳✳

That night, Ann was sitting next to her drawing equipment in our studio, crying. Out loud she says,

"I can't seem to stop thinking about you, Wayne. Everything I do and create has a part of you in it. It feels like it's getting worse every day and I'm not sure if what I am going through is even normal! Please, Wayne, help me! I need you!"

Her expression seems to somehow calm while she forms a slight smile on her lips. "Wayne, is that you?"

Ann feels that, somehow, Wayne's spirit is with her. She never believed in any form of ghost spirit in the past and wasn't about to change her views. Then again, she never thought she would be in a position to consider that once she and Wayne had met. Now, all of a sudden, she was finding herself hoping beyond hope that the idea of a spiritual afterlife might actually exist after all.

Although she continued to cry, she was maintaining a sense of contentment if only for a brief moment.

"Oh God! Wayne, I love you so much! Please, why did you leave me Wayne? Why did you go away from me, I love you!"

Gently, she lies down and slips into a deep sleep, one that she has not experienced in quite some time.

In her dreams, Ann sees Wayne standing before her, warning her he says to her, "You are in danger baby, and you need to do what Rick suggests. Please listen to him! He knows and wants what is best for you. Go on with your life and know that I will never lose your love for me, no matter what! Sleep now baby, and know that it's ok to dream."

The next day, Rick has returned to Ann's home and had already gone through the paperwork in the envelope. He found the copy of the photographs that were taken by Louie and Antonio that Wayne had managed to confiscate prior to leaving Michigan. He had recognized the gentleman in the pictures and realized the caliber of danger that Ann and her family are in.

The names of Louie Santino and Antonio Camboni were hand written on the back of the photographs as were the names of both the senators. Enclosed in its own envelope, he discovered a letter addressed to a Mr. Lucas Cavallari, a name he hadn't heard in a very long time. Later, Rick would find himself at the local library accessing Michigan public record files through the internet and discover that Louie and Antonio each have a long list of criminal arrests. Not surprising, he would also find that they are both deceased and had been buried back in New York. Rick took this opportunity to utilize Ann's computer to access the internet to investigate the current whereabouts of both the Michigan senators.

Senator Friese was a Democrat that came from a long family line of politicians. Unfortunately, and to his families dismay, he had also been dealing with issues regarding his assumed power and an obsession that he had with small children, information that had not only been buried but also covered up by his family over the years to protect their name.

Candidate McKnight, a Republican was known in the family for his ability to provide special favors for those who might deliver a favorable return, namely an endless supply of cocaine. In the past, he had done Frankie the favor of "making sure" that his desire to obtain a piece of property in order to open a family restaurant went through for a favorable return to satisfy his addiction. This property became the current location of Frankie's Italian restaurant with a mortgage that is now paid in full. Additionally, both senators were overlooking the drug money running through the club and the mafia by paying off the police commissioner, Michael Santino, Frankie's nephew and godson. All in all, the mafia had a pretty good deal going so their anger toward Ann's husband was certainly not unwarranted.

This information confirmed Rick's suspicions that The Bone Breakers as well as the mafia were attempting to gain full control over Michigan. Both Senators continue to be in power, suggesting to Rick that the Cosa Nostra did, indeed accomplish full control over the state. However, because Rick had found the photographs and documents, the power they had could be destroyed by Ann and one phone call to the Attorney General of Michigan. At this point, Frankie and Guido must be aware of the evidence that Wayne had in his possession. Rick was now convinced that Wayne was not hit by accident but had been, in fact, murdered. This meant that the Cosa Nostra had likely assigned associates to get rid of Ann and her family and would now be after him, since they must be aware that the evidence gathered by Louie and Antonio so many years ago was in Wayne and now Ann's possession.

Rick then begins to investigate the accident that occurred on October 3, and finds that the decedents name was Kay Montgomery-Cavallari of Detroit.

"Ann" he says, "take a look at this. I pulled up the accident at the location you gave me and the name of Kay Montgomery-Cavallari pulls up. She has a birthdate indicating that she would be the same age as Wayne, right? I thought that she and Wayne were married at the time of her death. But Ann's last name is Moore, not Cavallari."

"That's ridiculous," Ann said, "you must be looking at

different case. What was the other information you were looking at?"

"I was checking on the political status of Michigan. If my assumptions are correct, the mafia and the Bone Breakers have every reason to be after your husband and now, I'm afraid, you Ann."

He pulls up Ann and finds that her maiden name was Smith and her married name is definitely Moore. "This can only mean, then, that Wayne had assumed a false identity and was given the name of Lucas Cavallari at birth." He told her. "Look, Ann. I believe that this whole situation is going to be filled with information that you knew nothing about. But that doesn't mean that he didn't love you any less. As a matter of fact, you should be looking at this like he loved you more than any man is capable of loving a woman. He was protecting you from some very, very bad people."

"Can I offer you some coffee?" she politely asks attempting to avoid the truth.

"I would, um…black with a teaspoon of honey? Thank you."

Ann fetches the coffee and they retreat to the patio. "Now, what do you think is going on? I can tell that you're thinking something, Rick. You don't need to be uncomfortable with me, or even hide anything from me. I think I can take this."

"You're going to need to sit down for this. I was aware of your husbands name a long time ago. I just found out through my quick little research in there that Wayne Moore was really Lucas Cavallari."

"Your maiden name is Smith, is that correct?" He asks.

"Yes".

"Well, the individual involved in the accident at the location described in your husbands' paperwork was named Kay Montgomery - Cavallari. She was married to Lucas Cavallari, both from Detroit, both born in 1964, and both residing at the address that your husband filed taxes under prior to her death. This means that your name is not Moore, but is Cavallari and that your husband's first name was not Wayne, but Lucas."

Ann is sitting down, holding the arm rests of her chair with a look of shock on her face.

"Ok, wait a minute! Do you have *any* idea what you're talking about? Where are you getting this information from, Rick? How dare you accuse my husband of lying to me?!"

"I'm not accusing him of anything! I'm telling you that I checked into public record and found that the individuals involved in the accident were reported as Kay Cavalleri and Louie Santino. There is absolutely *nothing* supporting the name of Kay Moore. Now, you can check it out for yourself, or I can stop helping you right now. This is obviously too upsetting for you, Ann, and my intention is not to upset you, but to give you the facts, like you indicated you wanted. I'm only trying to help!"

"How can that be? I know that Wayne would never lie to me. How do I know that what you say is true, Rick?"

"I am so sorry Ann. I may have further information as to why your husband changed his identity. You can either believe me, or not. Hell, you can even check this out for yourself. I pulled it up on your computer Ann in a matter of seconds. Ann, I knew your husband a long time ago. He had come up as deceased many years ago, so we all just let the name rest along with him. This information puts you in some serious danger, Ann, and if I tell you this, you're going to have to understand that, as a cop, your level of danger is that much greater."

"I'm sorry, Rick. Please, go ahead with what you found. Just don't expect me to be okay with all of this, it is quite a bit of information you're expecting me to absorb right now, and I'm not so sure you could handle it any better than I am."

"When he was much younger, your husband was a member of a very powerful club in Michigan called the Bone Breakers. This club is not only very well known throughout the United States, but is also directly involved with the mafia. Their intention was and still is to assist the mob in obtaining as much power over the state as they could until they had full control. What I mean is that they wanted full political power. In so doing, they had hired two individuals to obtain blackmail information on the state senators. More specifically, this 'hiring process' was conducted by your husband. This information was in Wayne's envelope that you handed me." Ann is staring at him incredulously as Rick continues, "I can show you all of Wayne's real credentials as well as the pictures proving what I am telling you."

Ann holds up her hand for him to stop. "Louie", she repeats, "Is that the guy that Kay was having the affair with?"

"The very same." Rick returns. "Louie and Antonio were both murdered executioner style, their bodies were discovered by accident in an open field by a construction company months later. Kay was forced off the road in her vehicle. There was also a photograph in the file of a second set of tire tracks found at the scene of the accident of which I can only assume that Wayne obtained himself or stole from the crime file. It's possible that the mafia knew Wayne had this information. If his identity was somehow disclosed to them, then they could also have been made aware that the explosion was staged. I'm fairly certain, Ann that they were directly involved with Wayne's death."

"My God, Rick! That means that the two men running from the scene of Wayne's accident were actually members of the mob?" Ann asks.

"It would appear that way. I haven't been able to get any information on them yet, but I am working on it." He tells her.

"I can start looking from work. I will also to speak with Jack about this. He and Wayne have been friends forever and had moved together from Michigan. So, if Wayne had a different name, then Jack might have too." Ann suggested. "By the way, Rick, how do you know so much about all of this? You didn't have time to do that much research while you were on my computer."

"Because I, too, am a member of the same club. Although I am technically retired, once a member always a member, until the death."

"Then you knew my husband?" She asked him

"I believe I did. You showed me a picture of him, but I didn't recognize him. He likely had surgery to disguise his features so that no one would ever be able to identify him. Somehow, the Cosa Nostra *and* the Bone Breakers had an informant to identify him."

"But after all these years?" Ann asked him, "why would they wait so long? It seems to me that they would want to get rid of him as soon as possible, not wait this long to take care of things."

"And, you know that does make sense, Ann." Rick told her, "but the problem is that the power these people want is to a caliber that you may not be able to understand. Hell, I don't understand it. That's why I retired. They are very powerful people and are absolutely relentless. The mafia holds grudges for generations. You know that!"

She did. Although she had never done much research on the organization, it was fairly universal knowledge that the mafia was unforgiving.

"At any rate, don't get Jack involved in any of this. At least not yet. All of this could jeopardize his life as well as furthering the danger of your own. Please don't underestimate these people. I know a whole lot more than you realize and a few of them personally. These are not people that you want to challenge in any way. You really don't know who to trust right now and if the wrong individual sees you working on this, they could report to the wrong person. Don't forget, the mafia is filled with people of all walks of life, cops included, Ann."

She knew he was right. There were many members that had various professions to hide their real interest, and police officer could very well be one of them.

"I have just been informed that the man of my dreams was not only involved with the Italian mob, but that the man of my heart and soul, is not who I thought he was. I have been living these past few years in one of the worst lies I can think of!"

"True…but that does not change what you felt for him, does it? His name is different, but you knew him and developed a very strong bond with him. If we are going to clear this up, I need you to be with me, not self absorbed into his past. Whether you called him Wayne or Lucas is completely irrelevant. I don't think you're safe here in this house, Ann. Do you have anywhere else you can go?"

"Um, I'm not sure. Let me think on that one, ok?"

Suddenly Ann remembers a dream that she had the night before; something about a warning from Wayne. Quickly, she dismisses the thought.

"Come here." He holds his arms out and embraces her. She leans against his chest with tears streaming down her face. "Look, Ann, I know that you have received some of the worst news imaginable. However, I know you well enough now to know that you are a very strong individual and can handle this. Let's get going together on this investigation and keep your mind off of things. I want you to stay at a friend's house that I know of for now. He has an extra room there that you can stay in with all the accommodations necessary for you to be comfortable. The boys stay with me and my son, Joey. We'll drive by your house periodically. I think if you split everyone up, the likelihood of any of you being in danger is less, does that make sense to you?"

"Yes." she replies. "I have a good friend close by that will take the animals to her house. Are you going to bring the boys to me so I can see them?" Ann was thinking of asking Sharon to watch the animals for her.

"Ok…but let's keep this quiet at least for a few days. We don't need their safety jeopardized."

"I'm gonna have a beer, do you want one?" She asks.

"Can't. I am allergic to wheat!" He chuckles and Ann follows suit. "How about a Whiskey and soda?" He asks, smiling

"Coming right up." She gets up to go into the house to fetch the drinks. He follows behind, gently turns her toward him and kisses her fully.

"I'm sorry Ann." he says after they disengage, "I hope I am not overstepping my bounds."

"Please Rick, I'm not ready for that yet, okay?" she says, tears begin to soak her face. "I promised myself to Wayne for the rest of *my* life, not his! As far as I am concerned, he and I are married for an eternity. For you to expect me to begin any intimate relationship would mean in my heart that I am being unfaithful."

He takes a step back from her. "I understand, I hope you can forgive my intrusion. I guess I can see now how the man fell in love with you right away. You must be the strongest woman I've ever met in my life. There are so many things about you that I find attractive that I guess I let my feelings get the best of me, is that okay?"

"Yes, I suppose it is. I'm glad you can understand and I don't want you to take this to heart. I can't imagine myself with anyone else, nor do I want to."

✳ ✳ ✳ ✳ ✳ ✳

When Luke received the news so many years ago about his wife, he went down to the county morgue to identify her body. After discovering the second set of tracks at the scene of the accident, he did take photographs of what appeared to be a second set of tire marks. Knowing that he and his best friend Tony were in immediate danger, they both packed as quickly as possible, instructed Lucas' parents of the staged death and left the state, unsure of where they would end up.

Luke was at work that day when an officer walked up to him to deliver the news. When the officer walked into the warehouse, he was wearing a minister's collar. Luke knew immediately that something was desperately wrong.

They both had already filed for the divorce, but Luke continued to maintain his feelings for her. After the officer informed him of the accident, his presence was requested at the morgue to identify the bodies. Following the verification of his wife's death, he drove directly to the scene of the accident where he had snuck a picture of the marks on the road since the accident meant that all three individuals involved with the incriminating evidence were dead. He never brought the accident up again until Ann asked about it and even then, they only discussed it briefly. Although Ann has been a cop longer than they had been married, she never investigated him.

The following evening, Rick and Ann headed into Wayne's office to go through more of his belongings. Ann still had the envelope given to her by Jack that showed the names of the individuals on the hit list. She was not yet ready to disclose this to Rick, the list showed that Wayne most certainly had some information that could likely have led to his death. As their appointed hit man, Wayne had apparently maintained this information and, possibly, had even forgotten about it. Ann knew that Wayne's past was placed on the back burner from the moment he met Ann in order to protect her, she also knew that he was thinking of her as his last conscious thought.

Should the information they found have been discovered by the mob, both of them might be in some very serious danger as these documents could tie the club and the mob to various murder cases. Was it possible that they knew Wayne had copies of all this information and that is why these events are occurring? As a cop, Ann knew that every scenario receives doubt before benefit, therefore it is necessary to analyze the worst case scenario which is what she was doing. Then, if that is true, Jack knew more than what he shared with her that day. Rick had more information on the goings on with the club as a retired member, and Cosmos was a true killer. This also meant the she and her boys were in some very serious danger because she must assume that the mob knew of the pictures and documents and that Ann had all the information to destroy their plans to obtain power. This was huge and now Ann must find a way to protect her boys, herself, and the rest of her family.

Louie and Antonio were long term members that had built a strong trust with Frankie Sarducci, the leader of The Bone Breakers and head of the Mafia in Detroit. As two of his most trusted members, they were both capable of establishing inside information that Detroit's rival club could use to obtain overall power of the state.   Once the head of the mafia has reason to believe that a member was betraying them, it wasn't likely that anyone would actually confront that individual. Not, at least, until they knew for sure that their suspicions were correct. Because Wayne was responsible for both organizations, it was his duty to follow any associate suspected of betrayal, establish the facts and take care of the situation.

One evening, Wayne had followed Louie and Antonio to the rival clubs turf and discovered that they were making arrangements to receive large sums of money for cutting all bags of crystal methamphetamine sold by the Bone Breakers with baby laxative so as to make the club lose their credibility with the drug dealers and users. This would cause the club to lose business so that Louie and Antonio would be able to take over the drug profits and, therefore, obtain full control. Additionally, they had pictures and documents on the senators that placed both men under the mafia's control to avoid destruction of their status with the public. The information they had was enough to destroy all credibility not only of the senator's but their family line as well.

Wayne had informed Guido in New York of the goings on so as to protect his status and allow the relationship between the mob and the club to continue. Guido was told about the information collected by Louie and Antonio, the drug tampering and the deal that was being made behind Guido's back with his drug supply. All of this information was pertinent to the success of the club and the mob in Michigan and, if it wasn't handled, could have an effect on New York as well.

Because Ann and Wayne were so close, it would be safe to assume that Ann might have knowledge regarding Wayne's past, making Ann a definite threat to both the mob and the club even though Ann had no idea that the club Wayne was involved in was helping the Mafia with corruption in the state.

What Ann did not understand was how they might have obtained information regarding Wayne and his present location after all these years unless, possibly, "Laurie!" Ann said out loud.

The only person Ann knew of that might have made the connection regarding Wayne's erroneous identity would have been a girlfriend that left him with a rather nasty break-up. One evening, before the boys were born, Wayne and Ann were discussing parts of their past. He brought up a bad relationship that he had become involved in and disclosed information to Ann that he had never told anyone else. This was the one and only time that he had offered so much information regarding this woman because of the horrible things she did to him and his embarrassment at falling for it.

Her name was Laurie Hartman and the two of them were co-habitants for a very brief period of time. So brief, in fact, that Wayne never even considered their relationship to be anything more than a cry for attention. They met at a program for drug addicts and Wayne believed that Laurie, too, had an addiction that she was trying to overcome. While in Michigan, Wayne had become dependant on drugs and made a decision to get rid of his habit once and for all following a bad episode.

He had gone on a trip lasting three days that he had no recollection of. Apparently, he had gotten carried away to the point of blacking out. When he woke up the following morning after returning, he decided that his addiction had gotten the best of him. This drove him to the decision of getting rid of the addiction before it was too late.

Since he had just lost Kay and was going through an addiction problem, he discovered later that Laurie used his vulnerability to feed her own desires. Laurie had, earlier in their relationship, asked Wayne numerous questions about his life in Michigan. It led to his telling her that he was working, indirectly, for the mob. A mistake that he regretted for some time to come. The day they separated, Laurie sold Wayne's motorcycle without his knowledge and had left that same day never to be seen or heard from again. A couple years later, Ann and Wayne had attended a funeral and Laurie had shown up.

It had been years since Ann had seen Laurie, but she was confident that she would recognize her if she were to run into her again. Ann picked up the phone to call Jack.

"Hey Jack." Ann said when he answered. "I was wondering if you could come by for dinner tomorrow evening."

"Sure!" Jack responded, "I'll be there about six".

"Great! See you then!" Ann hung up and dialed Rick.

"Can you come over right now?" Ann asked.

"I'll be right there. Are you okay?" He asked her.

"Yeah. I have something I want to talk to you about."

A short time later, Rick arrived at Ann's house. Sitting down to the kitchen table, Ann talked while she was cooking up a homemade spaghetti sauce.

"Smells great!" Rick said.

"Good! I hope you brought you're appetite! Dinner is about served." The four of them ate their dinners and, when excused, the boys ran off to get their homework done.

Sitting down to a glass of wine for each of them, Ann began to tell Rick of the history of Wayne and why she felt that Laurie may be the key to all of this.

"You haven't seen her since that funeral?" Rick asked.

"No," Ann replied, "But she is the only possible person that could have known that Wayne, Lucas, was still alive. See, his parents moved here a couple of years after Wayne did. I don't know why I never thought of this before, but Laurie and Wayne met right after he moved to Arizona. I didn't meet his parents until much later when I became pregnant with Phillip. The Moore's must have found out about his location and come to visit him. Laurie could have somehow found out that they were coming to Arizona on vacation and followed them at that time. It would make sense since they only came to visit once before they moved here."

"But why would Wayne have told them about his location so soon after?" Rick wanted to know.

"I don't know. Maybe he wanted to reassure his parents that he was okay and wanted to see them. Maybe he thought that his death was real enough that everyone believed him. I don't know, but what I do know is that Laurie is the only person that could have found out about Wayne and where he was living."

"Then you do believe that this is all a set up?" Rick asked

"Yes, Rick, I do. I think that Wayne was in more trouble than he realized and that his parents, our children, myself and everyone I know are also in some serious danger, including you."

Born in Michigan, she was raised as an only child by a father who was a very determined, stern figure in her life, her mother had abandoned them both prior to her first birthday. Not allowed to venture out much past her daily outings to school and immediately home, Laurie led a very isolated life. He beat her almost regularly for crimes of which she did not see purpose such as unmade beds, towels hung sloppily in the bathrooms, and even failing to get dinner on the table. Laurie knew that her father was initially acting on his sorrow for the loss of his wife, but the anger and aggression turned into what she felt was an obsession.

She learned to hate her father and was anxious to rid herself of his company as quickly as possible. Determined to never marry nor to ever have a man corrupt her life, she wanted to have a child of her own to bring up in her own way. A way in which she could maintain control of another life just as her father did hers so she would do anything possible to make this happen. As far as she was concerned, a man's only purpose was to make her life comfortable and full of riches.

At the age of 18, she graduated from high school and shortly thereafter found a studio apartment that she could afford with her small wages made from a waitressing job at a local café. As a small child,

Laurie decided that she would never have a man in her life again. By twenty-one years of age, she had found a man who would make the mistake of bedding her only so that she could have a child of her own. Having made the choice to never see him again, she was determined to raise her son alone so as not to have the input of some stupid man to corrupt her beautiful new child whom she would name Ralph.

At the age of twenty-five, Laurie had obtained a job waitressing in a local restaurant run by an Italian named Frankie Sarducci. Frankie's "family" immediately took her in as her own and promised to teach her things that she could "never learn in school". They began to give instruction on small jobs such as hiding income from sales for the restaurant so they did not show a profit, only loss. She noticed that there never were many customers outside of the regular members. Frankie always sat at the same table with the same group of men and, occasionally, she would have one or two other small families to serve, but, it paid the bills and that was all she was concerned with.

Laurie became very close with Frankie and the others in his group and, soon, had developed their trust enough for her own assignment within the family such as finding some individual that had skipped out on a job, or possibly an addict that had not made good on his debts.

Then, the family was informed that Lucas had died in a mysterious explosion, however, everyone knew that his family continued to reside in Michigan. She was to find out if they were still in town and to get information from them regarding their son, Lucas. She was told that she could come up with her own method as long as they didn't discover her true identity. Well disguised, she headed out to watch the Cavallari family.

The couple were the only two known to be living in the house, Laurie approached them to introduce herself as they were loading up their vehicle with some suitcases and various other items. Pretending to be a concerned neighbor, Laurie approached them.

"Are you all moving?" She asked.

"Who are you?" The man asked

"I'm your neighbor from up the street. I work so much that I never had the time to meet you. Now, I see that you are going away and came to apologize for my own misgivings. I brought you a home-made pie to welcome you. Now, I suppose I will present this to you as a going away present! May I ask where you are going?"

"We're taking a trip to Arizona, not moving there" the woman quickly replied.

"Well, I'm Laurie. I can keep an eye on your house while you're gone if you'd like. You know, to make sure no moving vans pull up."

"Thank you. That would be fine." Tom told her.

"I'm Tom and this is my wife, Maggie." He told her.

"Are you going there to see the sites, or to visit family?" Laurie asked them.

"A little of both," Maggie replied.

"Well, here," Laurie said handing her the pie, "You can snack on this while you're traveling!"

"Thank you!" Maggie replied, "that's very sweet of you!" Taking the pie, Maggie turned to get into the vehicle.

Returning home, Laurie quickly called Frankie, "Do you know if the Cavalleri's have family in Arizona?"

"Not that I ever heard of, why?"Frankie asked

"Because they are heading out to Arizona to visit family right now, so if you want me to follow, I can head out right now."

"Get going and call me from a pay phone when you get there. I'll wire you some money for clothes for you and the boy."

"You got it!" Laurie hung up the phone, grabbed Ralph and the two of them headed out to follow the Cavallari's.

✳✳✳✳✳✳

Arriving in Arizona, Laurie sat back while the couple hugged some man she had never seen before.

"Wow," Laurie thought, "cute!"

She wrote down the address and left to find a pay phone.

Frankie answered as she told him what she had just witnessed. She told him about how they had both hugged this man as if they hadn't seen him in a long time.

"Go ahead and get yourself established Laurie. You have a few thousand waiting for you to pick up. Get an apartment and report to Santino's restaurant downtown where you will be working as a waitress. The owners name is Don Santino, he's expecting you. Call me when you get everything taken care of.

Her assignment was to pose as a drug addict wanting to rehabilitate.

Because of the mafia's interest in drug transactions, she figured that this would be the perfect place to make a name for Frankie with the drugs she planned on selling them at a fairly marketable price. She smiled at the thought.

At her first meeting, she saw the same individual that the Cavalleri's were hugging the day she was spying on them. He had been keeping to himself for the most part so she decided to introduce herself in the hopes of getting to know him and find out if he was, in fact, Lucas Cavalleri.

At their first break, she found him at the refreshment table and approached him.

"Hi! You looked like you were sitting by yourself so I thought I would introduce myself to you. My name is Laurie, Laurie Hartman. What's your name?"

"Uh, it's, uh, Wayne. Wayne Moore." He stammered

"Nice little party, huh?" She whispers to him.

"Uh, yeah, I guess. Look, I really don't feel well and am not really into talking right now. Will you please excuse me?"

"Yeah, sure. You're not really *into* this whole thing, are you? I mean, is it really helping you out? 'Cause I was going to go sit outside for a bit and have a cigarette. Care to join me?" She asked with an odd smirk on her face.

"Actually, I don't smoke, but I guess I can go sit outside with you."

They relocate to the front entrance of the building where the smoking section was located. She seems to take on a completely different demeanor than she had inside. Something about her, he thought.

They carry on a rather enjoyable conversation when, suddenly, the doors open and people begin to poor out of the building.

"Oops!" She laughs and he joins her, they had apparently talked through the entire meeting.

"Do you feel rehabilitated?" She asks.

"Oh yeah!" He exclaims. "Much better than when I walked in!"

The next evening, they both meet again. Again, they find themselves out front smoking. She had already planted the equipment inside, so this was her time doing her own investigation.

"So, Laurie, what do you do for a living?" Wayne wonders.

"Oh! I'm just a waitress at a little 'dive' over in Glendale. The food isn't very good, but my son Ralphie and I get by with the little bit I bring home. What about you?"

"Actually, I'm a welder and work for a motorcycle company building custom motorcycles. We do all different types of designs. I can show you some different things that I have done if you want." He offers.

"Maybe someday. That's not really my thing. Does it pay pretty good?"

"I do well for myself." He replies.

"Oh, good!" She says, knowing that she just received the answers she wanted. She hates this state. There aren't very many men that make decent wages here, so it becomes tough for a girl like her who just wants someone to provide for her and her son. Frankie was supplying her with more than she needed, but because of her youth, she learned that there is no such thing as too much money, so if this guy could provide for her while she was here, she and Ralphie would be rich one day.

＊＊＊＊＊＊＊

Over the next month, Wayne and Laurie begin to spend a significant amount of time together. They went to meetings, took her child to the zoo and movies all the while finding himself more and more drawn to her. Within a month's time, they found themselves living together.

Almost immediately following their co-habitation, They're relationship began to struggle. Laurie had discovered that Wayne didn't make very much money after all. Still, she wanted to maintain her promise to Frankie so she began asking questions about his past and found that he was involved in a motorcycle club in Michigan *and* worked with the Cosa Nostra.

"How did you get away?" she innocently asks.

"I had to fake my own death. Don't tell anyone, but it was necessary to protect myself and my family."

After a short time, their lives had gotten to the point that Laurie just could not take it anymore.

"I thought you did well for yourself!" She hollered at him one day when he drug himself back in from work. Their financial situation was not as well for the three of them. Ralphie didn't get all the toys he wanted because Wayne would complain that he didn't have enough money and the bills were beginning to fall behind. She had left her job as a waitress on Frankie's orders. They were done with the program and Wayne was feeling better now that he was living his life drug and alcohol free. But no matter what he did, he could never make Laurie happy. When they first moved in together, he thought she was content with his income and able to accept him for who he was. As time went on, he had discovered that Laurie's attitude was beginning to change.

Wayne had purchased himself a motorcycle through his employer with the hopes that the two of them would be able to get away and spend some time together. He quickly discovered that was not the case as Laurie would have nothing to do with either him or his motorcycle. It seemed that all she wanted to do was spend time alone with her son who didn't like Wayne either. He had suggested counseling to her at one point.

"Are you kidding me? Why would I want to go share our personal life with a complete stranger, Wayne? We are not going to go to a counselor and that's final!"

He felt it wasn't worth arguing with her, so he let that go as well and began spending more and more of his free time away from his home on his bike. Then, one day when he returned from work, he walked in to find that both Laurie and Ralph had packed their bags and moved out. He had left his bike at home that day and decided to drive. Shrugging his shoulders and knowing full well that there was nothing to be done about it, he retreated to the garage to get on his bike.

It was gone! Laurie must have taken his motorcycle!

Wayne was not yet comfortable with obtaining any form of identification with the state, so he had not yet gotten his driver's license established. The company identification he had had sufficed to this point. Because of this, he had his motorcycle registered in Laurie's name. So if she did take it he couldn't report it as stolen so now he would never get it back.

After speaking with the neighbors, Wayne discovered that Laurie had sold the motorcycle while he was at work. She took the money and left, never to be seen or heard from again.

Laurie arrived in Detroit to attend a pre-scheduled meeting with Frankie Sarducci.

"I found your boy, Frankie!" She exclaimed.

"Where is he?" Frankie wanted to know.

"Give me my money, and I will tell you!"

Frankie handed her a roll of crisp $100.00 bills totaling $50,000.00. "Now tell me where he is!" He shouts.

"Alive and well in Arizona!" She replied with a huge smile on her face. She handed him a copy of their rental agreement.

"How do you know it's him?" Frankie asked.

"He *told* me!" She laughed. The entire family joined in with laughter and celebration.

Frankie will not go after Lucas immediately. He decided to let the heat from his failed relationship die down first, let the man re-establish himself, then go in for the kill. Lucas, Frankie concludes, is not going anywhere for a while, so he has time to do the job and make sure it is done right.

$* * * * * *$

We will introduce ourselves with the names we had at the time of our deaths, Tom and Maggie Moore. That makes sense, because that is how everyone knows us…now. We have been married for more than 50 years and have 4 beautiful children, 3 boys and one girl. As in most families, our youngest child is the one we have always felt a closer bond to. Out of no choice of his own that we can identify, our Lucas has had many difficulties thrown his direction.

Don't get me wrong, we love all of our children and cannot imagine life without them. Our other three are doing very well for themselves and have somehow been given a "dish of harmonious gift" in which our Lucas was not quite so lucky.

When Lucas met Kay, our thoughts were that everything was going to be fabulous for him. He finally met the one woman that would make him truly happy, something every parent wants and desires for their children. However, in Lucas' case, or maybe because of his environment, he made some choices that we were not exactly supportive of, but learned to deal with and accept all the same.

In October of their second year of marriage, Lucas' wife Kay, was killed in a car accident by losing control of her vehicle and running it off the side of the road. She had died instantly, or so authorities said throwing Luke into a severe state of depression. The night after it happened, Luke's best friend, Tony, approached us with information that Lucas would be staging his own death by way of an explosion.

"Just play along with it. You'll receive information when the coast is clear. By the way, you should know that identity is not only in the name."

"What? What is that supposed to mean? And when will all of this take place?"

As Lucas' father, I am not sure how to express my exact feelings at the time as the idea of pretending that our baby boy was dead simply did not make any sense to either of us. How do you pretend the worst possible scenario a parent can possibly imagine and be okay with that thought?

Not only had Lucas become very distant from us, but suddenly he was having his death staged by way of an explosion. He and Tony were working in a warehouse building and designing motorcycles using flammable chemicals. But why would our son stage his own death?

Years ago and during his involvement with Kay, Luke had gotten himself involved with drug use and had been exposing himself to individuals that were not exactly upstanding citizens. He became very secretive around us, something that he had never done before even during his teenage years.

Over time, his marriage to Kay became more stressful when he came to us one evening needing to talk. We both thought it odd that he was alone that evening. This had not been normal practice for him because since his marriage he and Kay were practically inseparable.

"There is something I need to talk to you both about. This is something I am not sure I know how to deal with and I need some advice. I'm not sure where to begin, so I think I will just come right out and say it. Mom, Dad, Kay is having an affair."

"How do you know? Did she tell you?"

"She came to me the other night and told me. She just openly admitted it, now she says that she's scared because this guy is real dangerous. She's everything to me, I can't even believe this is happening. All she would tell me is that this guy is a very bad person and if she breaks it off, she is afraid that he might kill her! I don't know what to do and was hoping that maybe you guys would have some advice for me."

"Lucas, you need to listen to me! I know how you feel about her, but she has been cheating on you! Don't you think that this is her problem now? Leave her! You can stay here if you need to, but let her suffer the consequences! I know that sounds awful, but as your father, I am telling you that this is her problem."

"I'm sure you're right, but what if what she is telling me is true? I can't live with that!"

"That was her choice and if she can't get out of it, what makes you think that you can?"

"I believe that what she is telling me is true. Yes, she did in fact screw up. But at least she told me about it. I know that was hard for her to do and that she *wants* to get rid of this guy, but she can't. So you think I should just divorce her even though I made a life-long commitment, right?"

"That life-long commitment did not include violating the Ten Commandments, honey. For God's sake, open your eyes! We love you and only want the best."

"I agree with you Maggie. Kay has committed a severe crime and has placed herself in harms way by her own doing."

Lucas has never defied his father's words. He then turns to leave. "Dad, you know I can't deliberately go against anything you tell me, this may be the first time in my life I have considered it. I'll call you both tomorrow, good night."

The following night, Lucas did call with news that neither one of us ever expected.

I answered the phone after the second ring.

"Hello?" I say.

"Mom?" Lucas' voice is shaking and he is crying.

"Honey, what is it?"

"It's Kay, mom! She's dead!" He begins crying uncontrollably.

"Baby! Try to calm down! Where are you? Are you safe?" I ask, my own voice faltering.

"I'm at home and, yes, I am safe. But Kay lost control of her vehicle on some black ice, her car flew off the side of the road, and the police say she was killed instantly. Mom, I had to identify her body because of the damage! Oh God! Mom!"

Tom and I load up in the car and get to Lucas as quickly as possible.

When we arrive, we find our son sitting on his couch with his face buried in his hands. I have never seen my child so hurt, with so much pain on his face.

"They say it was only an accident. I cannot believe that she is gone. How am I supposed to continue without her?" I have no idea what to say at this point.

Although both Tom and I find this entire situation a bit coincidental, we discuss the different possibilities. Tom invites Lucas to dinner that next evening as neither of us believe that he should be alone. "Son" Tom asks him, "Did Kay actually break her relationship off with this guy?"

"She said that she was going to, but when I asked her when, all she could tell me was that she would do it soon." He replied

"Did she tell you his name?" Tom asks him

"Yeah, she said his name was 'Louie', but I didn't get his last name. She might have told me, dad, but I can't remember what she said." Lucas lies. "Does it matter?"

"Maybe not, son. But if you can find out, that might be good information to have. I know this must be hard for you and recalling information on that guy is the furthest from your mind right now, but that information might protect you."

"Sure, dad." Lucas replies. "I guess there is a part of me that agrees with you. At the same time, I know that I love her with all my heart and am not sure that I can feel whole again. Umm, they were actually together when the car was found."

"Are you sure it was him?"

"Yes, sir." Lucas said to his father, "I knew what he looked like. Don't ask me how, ok?"

Following our son's staged death, we were able to visit him in Arizona to see what his new life consisted of. He had changed dramatically, had enrolled in a program to get rid of his drug and drinking habit and had cleaned up his life by getting away from those awful people he was hanging around in Michigan. Over time, we were able to move to Arizona so that we could be closer to him and his new family.

Ann was a wonderful person. She was the furthest from anyone we ever expected him to be with, though. She was working as a police officer and was the most beautiful woman we had ever seen.

The two of them had married and Wayne was working as a manager for a welding company. He had moved on with his life and had proven his successes.

All contact with his friends from Michigan was discontinued save for Tony aka Jack, who had relocated with him, and his life was back to the life we had always hoped for. He had admitted himself into a rehab program that seemed to be successful.

Prior to meeting Ann, Luke had dated a woman by the name of Laurie. She was highly intimidating, according to Jack who had claimed that she seemed not only controlling of Luke, but also very demanding. According to Jack, the two of them had a falling out and she took off with some of his property. As far as we were concerned, Luke was better off if this lady was everything Jack claimed her to be.

✳✳✳✳✳✳

Ann is staying at this friends' house, very nice people that were very gracious to have her there. Although she would rather be in her own home among Wayne (Lucas') belongings, their belongings, she cannot complain as the accommodations are far better than she had expected. She knew it important to maintain a low profile; however, having not spoken to Rick in a few days, the feelings of loneliness were unbelievably overwhelming so she did the best she could by hanging around Rick's friend Martha as much as possible.

Ann was not sure how to feel about all the information she had received as of late and, knowing that Wayne was living under a false identity, she found more comfort in Ricks' words that his identity does not matter. She knew him better than anyone else did and also knew that Rick would help her to bring justice to Wayne's murder. Then, Ann's phone rang.

"Hey there!" It was Rick's voice on the other end.

"Hey guy! I was just thinking about you!" Ann was delighted to hear a familiar voice. "Any news?"

"Well, yes. But I need to get together with you because talking over the phone is not safe."

"Ok. When and where?"

"Now and outside" He responds.

Ann hung up the phone and rush out the door to meet him as previously discussed. He gave explicit orders not to go out without a disguise. Clad with a black wig, and cheap framed glasses, she ran out to meet him.

"Come on, we are going out." He informs her as he led her by the arm to his car.

They headed out toward a crowded strip mall. Large crowds have a tendency to create more of a distraction.

"What's going on?" Ann asks, a bit nervous now.

"I just found out that one of your friends and her husband were murdered. Barbara and Steve ring a bell for you? It seems that the Cosa Nostra found out that you had a connection with them. They must have found out about your going over there to visit and figured that they had information regarding your husbands' past."

"Oh my God!" Ann begins to cry. "What do I do now? What am I going to do Rick?" She lays her head on his shoulder as he attempts to consol her.

Rick is doing his best not to overstep any boundaries with Ann. Having developed some strong feelings for her, he wants to maintain the trust and confidence that she obviously feels for him. To this point, she has no idea that he, too, has been widowed.

"We are going to find these individuals, I *promise* you that! I can't tell you how sorry I am to deliver this type of news to you. You just continue to lay low like you are. You're doing a fabulous job, Ann. I'm not sure I have ever met anyone with your kind of strength."

Ann knows that he is only attempting to make her feel better. But she has grown tired of hearing those words. She misses Wayne, dearly.

"I know you're trying to make me feel better, but ever since I lost my Wayne, I have heard from everyone that I *have* to stay strong. I am tired of being strong Rick. I just want someone else to endure the pain for me for once. How much more am I suppose to take? What am I *really* going to do now? If I have friends, they are in danger of being killed. What happens if I fall in love again? Does that person die on me too? Hell, it already happened to me twice in one lifetime, who's to say that it will not happen a third time?" She lets her face fall into her hands and continues to cry.

She can feel Rick's hand rubbing her back as he replies, "Who says I'm going to die on you?"

She lifts her face up to look into his eyes and for a split second, Ann can see the look Wayne used to have with a smile to "sink a thousand ships". Shocked and speechless, she lets him dry the tears that have soaked her cheeks. He places a finger under her chin, lifts her face to his and kisses her passionately.

Breaking away from his hold on her, Ann pushes Rick back and asks,

"Is this too soon? Shouldn't I still be in mourning, Rick? The guilt I feel right now is way too overwhelming! My plans were to be married to Wayne, Luke, until death do us part. *My* death, Rick, not just his."

"Why is that? Do you honestly think that he would want you to never love again? Do you believe that your feelings for him were never to continue if he could not be with you? Look, Ann, he *chose* the prior life that he led, just as he *chose* to ride his motorcycle that day. You had nothing at all to do with that. You don't have to discount his feelings for you, and you also don't need to discount your feelings for him. He will always be a major part of your life and so can I if you'll let me. He had an identity that he couldn't share with you, it sounds to me like that was only to protect you of which he did a pretty phenomenal job. You two loved a lifetime, you *told* me that! I believe that if you give yourself the chance, you might be able to love again to the same degree. Look, Ann, I don't expect you to give up your love nor your quest to find the real killer of your husband. I only ask that you not shut the door completely to me, ok? Just think about it." He got up to leave. "You gonna be ok tonight?"

"I think that I could, but will you stay with me a while longer?"

"You bet I will." He smiles as he returns to his seat.

Rick left about an hour later. Ann headed back to her room to prepare for bed and began thinking about everything that had happened to her over the past few months.

✳✳✳✳✳✳

The next day, Ann spent alone to take in all of the past events and to replay everything in her mind. She wanted to be alone to establish some sort of sense to her husbands' murder.

While in the midst of thought, she considered the prior events of the "near miss" accident and Cosmos who may have been involved somehow in both events. If the plate identification from the car that tried to force her off the road that night was registered in New York as the truck that killed Wayne was, maybe they could somehow establish a connection between the two.

She ran to the nearest payphone to call Rick.

When he picked up, Ann didn't say hello before she blurted out,

"Hi! I'm headed to the police station to look something up. Would you please meet me in an hour?"

"Sure" Rick replied, "what's up, Ann? Are you ok?"

"Yep. Just may have had a revelation, that's all. Meet me in an hour, ok?"

She ends the connection.

It was imperative that she get this information to Rick as soon as possible. The problem was that she didn't know Cosmos' last name.

Remembering that an acquaintance by the name of Tina had introduced her to Cosmos initially, she decided to take a chance on contacting her.

Gratefully, the line is picked up.

"Hello?" A female voice on the other end of the line answers.

"Is this Tina?" Ann asks

"Yes, who is this?"

"Tina, this is Ann. Remember me?"

"Oh, yeah, what do you want?"

"So you remember Cosmos? It's important that I get in touch with him."

"It's Sarducci. Cosmos Sarducci. He lives out in Mesa. He is my friend, Ann, and I don't like lies being made up about my friends!" She slams the phone down in my ear.

"Well," Ann thought, "that went well."

Dialing Rick's office number, there is only a message recording on the other end. She leaves a message for him to get in touch with her later that evening, leaving her agreed upon code name so as not to disclose any information.

That evening, Rick met her out front as had become common. She was starting to feel like some sort of phantom when she was with him. Disguises, meeting places, not exactly what she thought was a great foundation for a solid relationship. She missed their meeting location on her back patio. Meeting here seemed so impersonal.

Once Rick arrived, Ann immediately informed him of her discovery.

"He's about 45 or 46 years of age I would guess, about your height, with a sandy blonde colored hair. A mustache, no beard, skinny build with a 'sway-back' sort of posture. Jack said he knew him from Michigan, indirectly"

"What does that mean?" Rick asked her

"He told me he knew who he was but that Cosmos didn't recognize him. I think he is the one that killed Wayne and the one who forced me off the road."

"What makes you say that?"

"Because every time something happens, Cosmos is always in the background, somehow. Jack told me that he was involved in some bad stuff when they were in Michigan. Do you think it's possible that he is or was a member of the Bone Breakers?"

"I'll look into it, Ann. Was that the revelation you had for me?"

"That was it. I'm sorry, Rick, I'm probably just being silly now, huh?"

"Not at all, Ann."

"Also, I wanted to let you know that I really miss our meeting place."

"In front of the house?" Rick asked

"No, silly!" she said flirtatiously, "the back patio."

She could feel herself turning bright red as she smiled sheepishly at him.

Pulling her to him, he said, "Welcome back, kiddo!" and embraced her in a long passionate kiss.

Once the moment ended, they sat down to discuss the situation.

"Can you tell me exactly what happened that first night?" Rick inquired.

"Following Wayne's death, my friend Barbara, Jack and I had attended a motorcycle rally to promote the upcoming ride for Ann's husband when Cosmos and another gal we now, Tina, approached us.

You remember Jack, right?" Ann asked rick

"He was there when you and I met, right?" Rick asked

"That's him." Ann told him, "anyway, Tina politely introduced us and, after short conversation, had disappeared to converse with some other friends. Cosmos stayed with Barb and I, almost as if he were somehow attached. Tina had, it seemed, left without so much as a word, so suddenly, Cosmos became our problem. Anyway, Cosmos had a few beers and seemed fine, unfortunately, he followed all of us to my house where he continued to drink, until he was so inebriated that no one in their right mind would allow him to drive any vehicle home."

"How was he getting the alcohol?" Rick wanted to know

"From the little refrigerator out back, I guess. I never saw him get anymore alcohol, so maybe he was only faking it, I'm not sure. So, anyway, that level of comfort that seems automatic when people meet and begin a conversation wasn't there, but I guess I wasn't thinking about it at the time. I guess I was still so upset about Wayne that, maybe I lost my ability to care anymore. But as a cop, I knew my level of self preservation and dedication to the laws of the Judicial system, so having him follow me to my house was much more reasonable then allowing Barb the same danger besides, I had Jack to stay with me. Jack was my husbands' best friend, so I trust him to the end of the earth. Barb left and Jack and I drug Cosmos in to sleep on the couch. Sometime in the night, I awoke and found him in my room so Jack ran him off. Two nights later, I was run down by a 1970's sedan with a metallic primer paint job. That was the night that my ribs were broken and I made a report. I went down to the station and pulled his name up on the databanks. Let me tell you, Rick. This guy has a rap sheet a mile long. Burglary, auto theft, felony warrants, you name it, he's got it. It appears to be a bit too convenient that with all of these charges he isn't doing time, and there isn't an APB out on him. All of his crimes took place in New York and Michigan, go figure."

"Wow! You may be on to something!" Rick seems excited at a potential lead. "Give me the list of crimes and I will get back to you this evening. It's possible that I can find further information on this guy. Are you going to be awake for awhile?"

"What, you think I might be able to sleep for some reason?" Ann asked with a smile. "Thanks, Rick. Please let me know what you find out, if anything tonight, ok?"

That evening, Ann found it difficult to sleep. She couldn't seem to get the thoughts of Cosmos out of her head. It seemed too coincidental that both of these events happened so close to one another without there being some sort of correlation. Also, that he has so many charges and no recorded prison time. And what was he doing in Arizona if not to kill the Moore family?

Ann sits upright in her bed, "Oh my gosh!"

Grabbing the phone, she dials her father and mother-in-law.

"Hello?" comes a groggy male voice on the other end.

"Tom!" Ann exclaims into the phone, "are you guys okay?"

"Yes, honey. We are sleeping. Why are you calling so late?"

"I'm sorry, dad. I just had a bad dream and wanted to make sure you guys were okay. You are okay, right?"

"Yes, now go back to sleep honey, we'll talk to you later."

Tom hung up the phone. Ann knew that she was going to have to get some protection to them as soon as she could. She would call on her friend and fellow officer Chris to send him over there to watch them.

Later that same evening, Rick called Ann as promised.

"Well, Ann, you were right! Cosmos Sarducci is a suspected hit man for the mafia and a long-time member of the Bone Breakers based out of Michigan. It appears that his involvement with both organizations has been ongoing for a number of years. Not only were Cosmos and your husband involved with the same club, but it appears that Cosmos is a relative, brother, to a Frankie Sarducci of Michigan. Frankie is one of the leaders of the Bone Breakers and also a notorious member of the Cosa Nostra. This is pretty serious, Ann because this means that both organizations are after you, and the likelihood of a continual miss is not something you want to place bets on, if you know what I mean!"

"Wayne never actually gave me the clubs name so, until we found that information in the safe, I had no more information than you did. If the Bone Breakers' are a large organization like you say they are, why would they be interested in me? Or for that matter, why would they wait so long to come after Wayne and only *then* decide to get rid of me." Ann had never really associated with club members other than in passing. Even though Wayne was friends with a few club members and had been for years, Ann never got involved with what they did. Because of her line of work, their friends disassociated their "work" with friendly gatherings out of respect, Ann always thought.

It was no secret that not all motorcycle clubs were involved in crime, in fact, many of them were notorious for the charitable contributions they made to society. The academy instructed that most of this was in lieu of their actual activities, but that continues to be hearsay and Ann never chose to focus her attention on the possibilities. It was possible that Wayne's prior involvement had actually led to his own demise. Even though Ann knew that she should be angry with him right now, the only focus she was capable of maintaining was to find the killer or killers and have them punished.

"The way the mafia works is to lay low for as long as they possibly can before collecting on any debt they may have. Sometimes, their retaliation can take years. That way, their victims are not only left unsuspecting, but the police department's ability to connect them with the killing is less likely. Wayne had kept the information we found for some reason and the why is only an assumption at this point. These photographs along with the list of names that Jack provided you is reason enough for all individuals involved to come after whomever they deem likely to have inside information on the goings on within not just the mafia, but the Bone Breakers as well. If my assumptions are correct, Ann, you need to understand that they will stop at nothing to get rid of all parties *they* feel might have information. Those pictures we found alone are enough to put a few members away for life. Now, we have a full list of very important people that could likely be tied to prior murders or conspiracy cases. My assumptions are possibly the only lead going to protect you at this point. Honestly, Ann, that is my number one concern right now, protecting you and your children."

"I would like to get some protection to my in-laws as well. These guys most likely know where they're living and we have no reason to believe they might be safe." Ann told him

"Okay. Have you sent anyone over there?"

"Not yet, I wanted to mention it to you first. Then I was going to suggest sending Chris, a fellow officer I've known for years."

"That'll work." Rick said, thoughtfully

"How are Phillip and Andrew, anyway? I would really like to see them, Rick. It's hard for me not to get angry right now about being kept away from them!" At this point, she can only imagine how this entire situation would be upsetting to them both. But because she wasn't allowed around them, she had no idea how they were both holding up. Gratefully, she knows they are both too young to understand.

"How do you think they are getting through all of this Rick? Are they talking to you about it at all?"

"They are both coping very well. There is nothing for you to be concerned with. The boys are all hanging out together and have taken quite a liking to each other. It seems they have adopted many common interests." He reassures her.

"Oh, that's great. At least *something* is working out! I can't thank you enough for watching over and protecting my kids, Rick. That really means the world to me."

They hug and Rick offers to drive her back. Reluctantly, Ann replies, "I guess."

"What's the matter, don't you trust my driving?" He asks, apparently recognizing her expression.

"It's not that. Well, maybe it is, can I tell you something Rick?"

"Of course, Ann, what is it?" He asks

"I always told Wayne that he was my True North because I never trusted anyone other than him to drive. In my line of work, it isn't uncommon for any of us to try to get out of driving. Having said that, it is also not uncommon to distrust anyone else's driving. I know that must sound odd and possibly judgmental, but it took quite some time for me to be comfortable with Wayne's driving. Now, I'm back in the same position I was before."

"Ok, would you like to drive then?" he offers with a smile "it doesn't bother me, Ann. If you want to drive, go ahead."

"No, I hate driving. I left patrol for that very reason. When not working, I always made Wayne drive and, it is for that reason that he knows the area much better than I do! It's not easy for me to redirect myself to rely on someone else to get me from point A to point B, you know?" She is looking a bit embarrassed.

Rick pulls her to him. "Ann. I know that this is going to be hard for you when I tell you this. Have you eaten dinner yet?"

"No" she replies.

"Ok, let's go get a bite to eat. I think this will take a while."

Rick is about to tell Ann that he knows what it is to have the most important part of you taken away in an instant and for reasons that fall back on oneself. To have it taken away so abruptly that you find yourself doing whatever it takes to justify the incident.

They sit down at a rather elegant table in a high class restaurant.

"Rick! Are you sure about this place? It seems a bit expensive, don't you think?"

"Remember when you told me that you enjoyed the way Wayne spoiled you? What makes you think you aren't still worth that? Don't worry about it and please sit down. I have something I would like to tell you." He orders two glasses of wine.

"This begins a number of years ago. I was a bit reluctant to tell you about this. I thought you might think I was only trying to make you feel better."

He begins to tell her about his wife, Mindy, and how her life was taken in the blink of an eye.

"I'm going to start at the beginning, Ann, so there is no doubt about my past." He began.

"Good idea." Ann replied with not so much as a hint of humor.

"I used to live in New York and, like Wayne, was involved with the Bone Breakers. That doesn't mean that I knew any of the same people as your husband since I was simply a member and nothing more. Anyway, our chapter had absolutely no involvement with drugs, nor did they support drug use. One could pretty much guarantee that if they were caught with any drug activity, removal from the club was inevitable. During a meeting, we were all at a local bar and there were some individuals quarreling. A couple of us went out back to see what was going on when a shot was fired. There were two individuals that went down that night, one was critically wounded, another man was killed. When the police arrived witnesses were making statements that there were drug sales taking place of which I didn't know anything about, but I did see the shooting. The entire incident resulted in a big trial and because of my testimony, I went under the witness protection program. It was either that, or I could go down for other charges that I would rather not discuss with you at this point. I stayed under protection until after the trial. With my testimony, the chances of conviction were very strong, so authorities figured that I would be safe following the conviction. Long story short, two of the individuals were convicted for 3 years because they only got charges of accessory to the fact, the third who was the actual shooter was convicted for 25 years.

A couple of years later, my wife and I were celebrating our second anniversary; Joey was only a baby at the time. I had taken her to our favorite restaurant and, as we were leaving, a man walked up to me and said, 'Hey buddy! Remember me?' I didn't recognize him at all until he jogged my memory a bit. He was one of the individuals that I mentioned earlier, released on parole. He looked at me and said, 'I thought you might like to know how much it hurts to lose someone you love!' and he shot my wife right in front of me. The guy who got twenty-five years was his brother. Mindy died shortly thereafter from internal bleeding. He had severed her liver with the bullet. I was left to raise Joey alone. I never imagined that I would be able to move on with my life, Ann, but you know what? I found you and now I know I can. Following the entire episode, I discovered that I wanted to maintain my involvement with my brothers in the club and, well, here I am."

"Oh wow, Rick! I am so terribly sorry! You must think I'm a selfish person. I never expected that you might be experiencing the same thing as I am."

It was at that moment that they both felt a mutual connection that, perhaps, may end up saving both of them in the end.

✳✳✳✳✳✳

The Valente family has been maintaining full control over all of New York state for two generations now. An easy enough task, provided one keep tabs on the goings on around the various neighborhoods. Having connections in virtually every portion of Manhattan Island, Guido Valente was fulfilling his family legacy by controlling all illegal drug activity. Now, he had established his family and was in the process of controlling all of Michigan as well.

The state senate in Michigan as well as the Detroit police department were all his and that was where he was focusing on the dealings that were taking place. So far, the entire process was showing to be very lucrative. Senator Friese had become, literally, putty in his hands since Guido's associates had obtained information regarding his involvement with children. Unfortunately, the incriminating evidence was not yet, in their possession. Not a problem, the holder of the photographs was now found, a widow and living in Arizona. Shouldn't be much of a problem getting them back, after all, how much of a problem can she be?

His personal phone rang, the caller identification showing a call for his contact in Michigan.

"Hello."

"Hello, Guido! This is Frankie!"

"What do you want?" Guido asks with a hint of suspicion in his voice.

"Well, I have some news for you."

"What, Frankie?"

"We didn't get the broad yet. But," he stammers, "We think we know where she is!"

"What the hell is that supposed to mean? You *lost* her?" Guido asks angrily.

The only reason that Frankie has anything at all to do with Michigan is because of Guido's wife, Maria. Frankie is her youngest nephew and, as far as Guido is concerned, a complete buffoon. He has no ability to manage but there is no reasoning with Maria. The boy should be in an institution as far as Guido was concerned, but defy his wife's wishes and there would be pure hell to pay.

Guido wanted to send his brother Paul to Michigan, but as it turned out Paul had gotten pretty strung out on drugs. Because Paul has an extensive background in business management, that situation would have been ideal until Guido discovered that he had gotten mixed up in injecting his own drug profits. In the family, the cardinal rule of success is to maintain control of all drug profits, not to use them. So, Paul was no longer a potential candidate leaving Frankie as his only option.

Now, he is finding out that Frankie was proving his incompetence with the hit that Guido had assigned him. Somehow, Frankie managed to pull through on everything else. Getting rid of Lucas Cavalleri who betrayed both the club and the Cosa Nostra was foremost on his list, but allowing Lucas' second wife, Ann, to live simply would not do. She had the evidence that Guido needed regarding both senators. As irrelevant as many may think, that evidence pointed fingers at an entire lineage of corruption in office throughout Michigan and having it would mean that the Valente family would control both Michigan and New York for a very long time. Another issue of concern was that Lucas' present wife may have the evidence that tied the family to the murder of Lucas, his first wife and the two associates who managed to screw up the evidence collection in the first place. Since there is no statute of limitations on murder, Guido and the family could be charged anytime for any or all of the murders.

"What is wrong with you people? You cannot manage to kill a *woman?*"

"I'm sorry sir, but somehow she is getting help from another individual that she seems to have grown very fond of!" Frankie replied.

"Let me help you understand something and this is *not* up for negotiations Frankie! I gave you a simple task to carry out. Now I expect you to finish it! You get that girl and the evidence and I don't care what it takes. Then, you make sure you get this boyfriend *and* the cop! Keep in mind that we *are* on a schedule here and I don't plan to lose this one! You get the job done and do it right this time!"

"I will, Guido! I promise!"

Frankie hung up the phone and immediately contacted Cosmos Sarducci who was still in Arizona.

"Cosmos!" Frankie yells into the phone, "What's the status with the broad? Any luck finding her yet?"

"No sir. But we may have found something better." Cosmos returns

"What's that?"

"Lucas and Ann had two boys, sir. They are staying with this Rick guy and his son, Joey." Cosmos shows a hint of excitement in his voice.

"Are you sure?" Frankie asks

"Not yet, but we are watching him now. Sal has a micro-chip that he plans to install just as soon as we find the place empty and then maybe we can get something on tape. In the meantime, I have my boys watching them twenty-four-seven."

"Ok, but you need to hurry up. I got the boss on my ass about this now. He wants the broad and the boyfriend dead, yesterday. Go ahead and throw the kids into the picture as well!"

"You can count on me!" Cosmos replies.

"Hey Cosmos." Frankie retorts

"Yes sir."

"I just had an idea! Maybe we can get the broad to come to us if we have the four individuals that mean the most to her."

"You mean the boyfriend and the kids? Great thinkin' boss! We'll take them as hostages until you decide what to do!" Cosmos sounds real excited now.

"Be careful! I need this to go through without any mistakes. This could put us *both* in the 'big times' with the family, Cosmos!" They both laugh as they cancel the phone connection.

※※※※※※

Guido's office is located in the rear of his restaurant/dance hall in lower Manhattan. He has operated this same hall since he was old enough to work without attracting attention and, because he paid attention to his father, was rewarded with full ownership by his eighteenth birthday. He is fully staffed and receives a full house of patrons every evening.

In order to prevent bringing his work home with him, Guido had associates assigned to all necessary areas. This way, his stress level was lower and, once he left the office, he didn't need to think about work again. Now, he has such productive associates that he rarely has to go into the office. Until now, of course, the Michigan incident is causing a lot of issues. Until they get the evidence they need and close the Cavalleri issue, he would be on the clock continually.

Guido picked up the receiver of his phone and hollers to his secretary "Call my nephew, Frankie."

"Yes sir!" Responds a female voice.

In a few seconds, Frankie picks up the line.

"Frankie! This is your uncle. I want you to look up this Rick individual and get me some history. I have a feeling that we may be able to find some information on him, if you know what I mean."

"Already done!" Frankie replied "I found out that he is from New York. Remember Laurie the ex-girlfriend to Lucas? She looked him up and discovered that this Rick person now has some pretty strong involvement with the Arizona clubs and continues to maintain contact with the Bone Breakers. Then I found out that, back in New York he was held on accusations of killing a few members of a rival club but the case was thrown out of court as the charges were dropped. Anyway, the case in question was never closed, so the real killer has not been caught or, the real killer is Rick and he is being protected for some reason. Guido, the man that was killed was one of ours! That means that this Rick character stands a lot to lose if information gets out to prove that he is the real killer and all we really have to do, is plant some drugs and a bit of evidence on him. Now that we found him, we can kill two birds so to speak! Think of it as a kind of payback plan, what do you think?"

"Good job, kid! That will help me out a great deal! Have you made any of the arrangements?"

"Yeah! We got the equipment all hooked up. He and the kids are layin' low right now, but according to Cosmos it looks like Rick is getting ready to go out somewhere. He's getting awful dressed up! Oops! Gotta go! I'll call you in a bit, Guido!" And, with that, Frankie hung up the phone to answer the call on his cell from Cosmos.

"Hello?"

"Sir! This is Cosmos."

"Yeah, what have you got?" Frankie asks

"We're heading out to follow Rick right now. I think he might be going to meet up with Ann!"

"Right! Be careful and don't let him spot you! Call me back when you have something!" Frankie hangs up the phone.

****

Rick is getting ready for his hot date with Ann this evening. For some reason, he is feeling very nervous and not sure where these feelings are coming from since they have recently spent so much time together. It is possible that the feelings are coming from the fact that, next to Mindy, she is the one single person that he has confided so much information about himself to.

It hadn't been too long since Mindy's death and this will be the second time that Rick has gone out with a woman since. Ever since he met Ann, he has been thinking about Mindy a lot lately. Almost as if he is starting the process of grief all over again, he watches Ann with more understanding than she will ever know.

He remembers that he was told by so many people that they understood, and that he needed to be strong because that's what she would have wanted. Although he knew that they were only telling him what they thought he would want to hear, he did not want to be strong. All he wanted was to go curl up in a ball somewhere and disappear. All of a sudden, he was in the same position of those he resented so much to.

He has decided to take her out once again to a classy restaurant, this time in a very wealthy section of town. The boys were left at Rick's house playing video games and being kids.

"You guys gonna be ok?" Rick asks the boys.

"Sure dad!" Joey yells back. "Go have a good time! We'll just be hangin around playin video games!"

Rick smiles to himself knowing that his concerns were unwarranted. He was definitely blessed with a very bright, well mannered young man. He knows how lucky he is to have such an incredibly well-rounded son, especially raising him without a mother. Joey doesn't remember anything about his mom. He did begin to ask questions as he grew older but Rick and Joey always had a very good line of communication between them that did not seem to be lacking as far as Rick could tell.

Rick shows up at the designated meeting place to find Ann looking absolutely stunning. She is wearing a black evening gown, the like of which he has never before seen. Approaching her, he gives her a gentle kiss on the lips.

"My God! You look absolutely stunning!" He exclaims, unable to take his eyes off of her.

"You look pretty amazing yourself!" She reciprocates.

They head out to dinner and, upon arrival, Rick turns to Ann. "Let's make this time strictly for us, ok?"

"No business talk?" She asks with a gentle smile.

"No business talk, just us!" He replies returning the smile. She stops and continues to stare at him. Looking away, they both sit down to their seats.

"When you looked at me just then, I saw something." She stops with a look of confusion on her face.

"I don't know what it was, Rick, but for a brief second, you had that same smile that I remembered on Wayne the day I met him." She has an expression on her face that shows some kind of contentment, yet she looks as if she is about to cry. Not tears of sorrow though.

"It's ok, these things are normal."

"Are you sure? I guess that sometimes it feels like he's right here with me and then you do something that either acts or appears exactly like what he would do or express."

"You know, Ann, we are still working on this case and have yet to bring closure to what had happened to him. Why don't you just feel. Focus on that and that alone, and let your body do the talking. Eventually, you will come to the understanding that your life *will* continue. I think you are trying so hard to please what everyone else *might* think that you are forgetting about the most important person here and now. That person is *you*, Ann."

"I know, and I do hear what you're saying, Rick. I just can't seem to stop feeling that he is here and sometimes that he's showing himself through you. I know that sounds crazy, but it's true."

They finish their meals without much more conversation and get up to leave the restaurant. Outside, he pulls her over to him, she giving no resistance.

"Can we go someplace to be alone?" Rick asks her.

"Like where?" She inquires

"Like, I will show you. I have another 'special' place that I think you will like. We can sit, alone and no one will know where we are. Joey, Phillip and Andy are having fun paralyzing their minds with video games, so I am sure that they have no interest in us coming home. So, what do you say? Want to stay out past curfew with me?" Rick gives her an attempt at an evil smile. He knew that the boys would be okay with his house-sitter Joanna right next door. She often watched Joey for him and was a real life saver most of the time. She was a teenager that wanted the babysitting money and generally spent her time doing homework while Joey played his games. Rick had asked her to hang out at the house and play video games with the boy's while he was gone. He would end up returning home to find her asleep on the couch or curled up in the spare bedroom.

"I would love to!" Ann replied, laughing.

They head out to a remote area where they approach a cabin style home in the desert. Somewhat out of place, it had certain flair to it that Ann found comforting.

Ann had notified her friend and partner, Chris to have him swing by Rick's house to check on the kids if he found himself in the area. Chris would do anything for Ann.

Chris agreed, happily, and congratulated Ann on moving forward with her personal life. He was so happy to hear that she had happiness in her voice that, at this point, he would do anything to help her maintain that attitude. So, he agreed to go to the house to check on the 'guys' and make sure they were in bed and sleeping at a reasonable hour. Since he didn't live far from Rick, he would check on them first thing in the morning as well, leaving his cell phone number in case of an emergency.

After pulling up to the place Rick wanted to show her, he turned to her and announced, "This is my 'vacation' home. What do you think?"

"I like it!" Exclaims Ann. "Nice and cozy!" She announces as they enter.

"I haven't been here for quite some time, so I can't account for the appearance. Let me know if it is too dusty for you and we can find an alternative." Rick tells her.

"I'm sure it'll be just fine!" She replies as she begins to look around.

It was a real log cabin equipped with wood floors and out of date curtains covering the windows. It reminded her of a cabin her grandparents had when she was just a little girl. Her family would go there, she remembered, and stay for the weekend.

"You have an indoor bathroom I see." Ann announced to Rick.

"Yep!" He replied, happily, "I got rid of the outhouse just last week!" Laughing, he continues, "We thought we would actually put in glass for the windows, and electricity instead of the old Kerosene for lighting! It's a new concept, I'm pretty sure it'll catch on."

He grabs her arm to pull her close. They embrace in the most romantic kiss either of them has experienced in a very long time. He slowly begins to undress her and she him.

They spend the evening together repeatedly making love with more passion than either had felt themselves capable of in a very long time.

The following morning, as they are both preparing to face the day, Rick turned to Ann.

"Any regrets?" She faces him, smiles, offers him a passionate kiss and replied,

"None that come to mind, you?"

"Absolutely not!" He replies with his head held high and a slight grin.

He opens the door intending to allow her the respect of exiting the house first when, suddenly, he pushes her off to the side and slams the door shut.

"What is it?" She screams

"Stay down and be quiet!" He says in a hushed scream.

Rick crawls over to a living room cabinet. He opens the bottom door and pulls out his .9 millimeter automatic. He crawls back to the front door.

Startled, Ann says nothing but retrieves her weapon from her leg holster.

Outside, there is a dark green Cadillac parked in front of Rick's house. Ann captures enough of a glimpse to realize that it is possibly the same car that tried to run her off the road that night.

"Who is it?" Ann whispers to Rick.

"I'm not sure, but I think it may be our friends from the Cosa Nostra!" He whispers back.

"Which ones?" She questions

"The same ones that ran you off the road that night, I'm willing to guess. I would also venture a guess that they may be the same that killed your husband, Ann. I also think this goes much further than his first wife and not taking care of the blackmail issue. I will explain what I can later! Right now, please just stay down and *be quiet!*"

He crawls to the front window to peak out. Suddenly, a loud banging noise and glass flying everywhere. Rick quickly drops to the floor. He waits a moment and pushes himself up again to try and look out. Grabbing a quick peak, Rick dropped back down out of site once more.

"I can't get a very good view of them, but it looks as if there are only two. Here!" He reaches inside his Jacket and pulls out his .45 as he slides the 9 millimeter over to Ann. "Great!" Ann says, "Cover me!" She crawls on her stomach over to the rear door, looks out the window and slowly exits while maintaining her guard.

Inside, Rick hears nothing, but continues to look out the window while attempting to stay out of site. Finally, he gets a glimpse of what appears to be two men making a poor attempt to hide behind the vehicle. Waiting for an opportunity, Rick quickly moves over to the door that remains open just a crack.

Behind the house, Ann has stolen enough of a glimpse to convince herself that this is definitely the same vehicle that ran her off the road that night. Quickly, she retreats behind the house and depresses the emergency call button on her radio to alert the department of her whereabouts and that she is in trouble. Peering around the corner a second time, she is now positive that what she is looking at is the same vehicle.

Capturing a glimpse of one of the men, she realizes that it is none other than Cosmos!

"That little squid!" She thinks to herself. Cosmos was behind this after all. "But how did he know to come here?"

As quickly as the entire situation had started, it had come to an end. Ann heard two shots fired, then the slamming of a car door, the vehicles tires squealed and the car disappeared in the distance. Ann peaked, once again, around the corner of the house and saw Rick outside holding his left arm with his right hand. She runs for Rick.

"That was Cosmos." He said.

"I know" Ann replied, "Why do you think he was outside this house, Rick? We were careful, how did they know we were here?" Her voice was shaking.

"I'm not sure, but I think we better get to the kids, right now!" he said as he pulled Ann to her feet.

"You're hurt!" She exclaims. "Let me get something to dress your arm, a cloth or bandage, maybe? Rick, do you have any first aid items in this house?"

"In the hall closet next to the bathroom, please hurry Ann! I want to get to the boys and make sure they are still safe!" he has a very bad feeling.

Raising Joey alone, Rick had become very in-tune to what Joey was feeling. He always knew when Joey was sick or upset, almost as if he had a sixth sense. He had that same feeling right now.

"Ok," she said as she was heading toward the door. "Let's go. I will dress that on the way. Come on! You drive!"

Together, they raced back to Rick's house to look for the boys.

✳✳✳✳✳✳

Although quite some time had passed, Tom and Maggie continued to find themselves methodically functioning through their day after the loss of their son. They had spoken to Ann and had made it a point to maintain a strong relationship with her, yet they both found it difficult to accept the loss of their youngest child.

Early one morning, Maggie decided to call Ann to check on her and see how things were going. Wayne had been gone a while now and Maggie had grown accustomed to speaking with Ann on a routine basis.

Maggie picked up the phone and dialed, but there was no answer.

"Odd," Maggie thought to herself. She knew that Ann was always home in the mornings.

"Tom!" Maggie called to her husband "have you heard anything from Ann?"

"No, not since she last called. Why?" He shouted back to her

"I just tried to phone her and there was no answer. She's always home working in the mornings. Where is her cell phone number? I'm concerned, Tom."

"Oh, come on, Maggie" Tom replied with a hint of irritation "Maybe she decided to go out and get a life. Is there is crime in that? Call her cell phone, I'm sure she's fine."

"No, I suppose not" Maggie set the receiver down in its cradle.

Maggie was not accustomed to having anyone in her life that she does not worry about, especially someone like Ann. They both knew from the minute Lucas introduced them to her that she was an exceptional woman. Now that Lucas was really gone, they knew that Ann would always continue to be an important part of their lives. They both took to her immediately and considered her a second daughter.

Maggie knew that, until she heard from Ann, she would continue to worry for her well being. Although it was their son that they lost, they had each other to get through it, Ann had no one. They both knew that having the children with her was helpful, but she had no one that she could actually confide her feelings in. Maggie was pretty sure that, if Ann had gone to visit her family she would let Maggie know about it.

She couldn't help but worry and kept hitting the redial on the phone to attempt to get a hold of her daughter in-law.

Finally, Maggie received a call from Ann.

"Ann!" Maggie hollered, "Where are you? We have been worried sick about you!"

"Maggie, I think we may have found something, but I can't tell you yet. I'll contact you just as soon as I know everything's okay. Are you and Tom doing well? Have you seen anything out of the ordinary? Anything at all?" Ann sounds anxious and certainly not herself.

"No, honey, everything is just fine. Why are you acting like this?" Maggie asked

"I can't talk about it now. But as soon as I can, I will let you both know. Just be careful and I will call you when I can. Make sure you call me if anyone strange comes by, okay?"

"Okay, honey. Sure." Maggie replied hesitantly.

Ann hung up the phone, knowing that she had raised a suspicion in Maggie. Here intention was simply to make sure that there was no activity brought to them, yet. She knew that if these people could find she and Rick at the cabin, that they were serious about getting to her. What amazed her is that they hadn't gotten to her yet.

They were getting closer to Rick's house while Maggie was left at her own phone, blankly staring in disbelief. After a moment, Maggie walked into the living area to discuss the conversation with her husband.

"That was Ann." Maggie told him "somethings wrong Tom. She sounded awful strange."

"What did she say?" Tom asked her.

"She called to make sure that we were okay and to find out if we had seen anything strange." Maggie said to him.

"That's our little cop!" Tom said, dismissing Maggie's concern.

"That's it?" Maggie asked him "you don't find any of what I told you odd?"

"No." Tom replied, "she's a cop Maggie. That's what cops do."

Suddenly, there is a knock at the front door.

"I'll get it!" Maggie hurries to answer it.

The door is pushed open as Maggie turns the knob, and two men rush into the house.

Maggie lets out a scream as she falls to the floor.

"Shut up!" The man screamed as he used his foot to slam the door closed behind him. He raised his gun and pointed it at Maggie. "Check the rest of the house!" The man shouted

Turning, the other man ran from the front hallway into the living room of there home.

"Who are you?" Maggie asked just as the man pulled the trigger of the gun aimed at her head.

"Maggie!" Tom screamed just as the second shot was fired.

Then, there was silence.

∗∗∗∗∗∗

"9-11, what is your emergency please?" A nasal voice comes over the line.

"This is Mrs. Farnsworth on Depew Street."

"Yes ma'am, what is your emergency?" The nasal voice is sounding irritable now.

"I just heard a couple of noises that might have been from a gun."

"What is your address, ma'am?"

"17895 Depew St. Please hurry"

"Ma'am, I have a car on the way. What makes you think they were gun shots, ma'am?"

"I'm not sure but noises came from the house across the street. There was a strange car parked out in front of Tom and Maggie's house that I've never seen before." Mrs. Farnsworth replied

"Can you describe the vehicle, ma'am?

"A big car, I don't know the kind of car. It's big, that's all I know. It looks like it's a dark color, black or green I think."

"Ok, ma'am, I have an officer on the way, he will want to speak to you when he arrives."

"Ok, thank you."

Mrs. Farnsworth hung up the phone and hurried back to the front window to see what was happening.

The house was quiet when the officer arrived. As Chris walked cautiously up to the front door of the house, he raised his fist to knock on the door that quietly opened on its own. Gently pushing on it, there appeared to be something blocking the entryway. Chris side-stepped his way beyond the door where he discovered a woman's body laying face up inside the doorway with a bullet wound to her head. Chris continued into the house and discovered a male body in similar condition.

Both victims had been shot, executioner style and not too long ago. Both bodies were still warm. Calling for back-up, Chris continued his inspection of the premises.

Finding nothing else, Chris left the other officers in the house to collect evidence as he crossed the street to question Mrs. Farnsworth.

Mrs. Farnsworth answered the questions as best she could

"I called you as soon as I heard the noise. It sounded like gunfire to me," Mrs. Farnsworth told him "I didn't recognize the car out front, so I thought maybe something was terribly wrong. Are Tom and Maggie okay?" She asked him.

"Did you get a good look at the car, ma'am?" Chris asked her, ignoring her last question.

"I already told the officer that it was a big car, dark color, I think it was green. I'm sorry sir, but my husband was the one that could tell you what kind of car it was, what year, where it was made. Yep, he knew everything about them."

"Is your husband home?" Chris asked her.

"I hope not" she replied "he's been dead for the past ten years!"

"Oh, ma'am, I'm so sorry!" Chris said

"Really? You're a nice man. My Daryl was a pain in the butt!"

Smiling, Chris took her hand, thanked her, and returned to his car.

When they arrived at Rick's home, the front door was wide open. Entering, they found that the house was torn apart. Rick, gun in hand, allows Ann to conduct a visual inspection of the interior while he followed suit around the premises of the home's exterior.

While the entire house appears disheveled, there is no sign of the boys. Having possession of Rick's phone, Ann jumped as it suddenly rang. Grabbing the phone, Ann answered it.

"Hello?" She says. Then "Oh, thank God, Chris!" Ann shouts into the receiver

"Ann? Ann, what is it?" Chris asked

"I am at Rick's house, Chris. Both of the boys are missing! The house is completely torn apart and the front door was wide open when we got here! I haven't contacted the department yet, would you?"

"I'm on it! Any idea where they may be? Or where they may have been taken? Or by who? Jesus, Ann! I was there this morning and everything was fine. I am so sorry!"

"I have an idea that they may have taken them to my house. Rick and I are heading that way right now. I'll give you a call when we get close. Wait for my call before you send backup. I want to get there first, Chris."

"Ann!" Chris shouted "both of you need to be very careful! Get out of there and *wait* for backup! Ann, I just found your in-laws. They are both dead!"

"What?" Ann said back into the phone with a look of shock on her face. Rick turned to her

"What is it Ann?"

"Oh no!" Ann screams. "Chris just found Wayne's parents. Rick! They're both dead!"

Rick grabbed the phone from Ann. "Chris, what's going on?"

"Rick. Wayne's parents were both shot and not too long ago. You both need to get out of there, right now!"

"We're heading back to Ann's house right now, Chris. We have to find the boys! Joey, Phillip and Andrew were together and we can't find them anywhere. It stands to reason that they would head back to Ann's house. We saw some of them this morning at my cabin, Cosmos and another man, but they got away."

"Did you see the vehicle?" Chris asked him

"It looked like a 70's model Monte Carlo, green. Neither of us were able to get a plate on it, though."

"Okay, Rick thanks"

Ann took the phone from Rick, "Chris, we're pulling out right now, go ahead and send some officers, but tell them to hold back. If they pull up to the house, these guys might hurt the boys."

"You got it, and Ann."

"What is it?"

"Hang in there, everything is going to be fine. I promise."

"Thanks Chris." Ann hung up

Chris knows Rick and Ann both well enough to know they won't wait and that they are going to do what they can to get their kids back so he called his partner on the cell phone.

"Jim," Chris said, "do me a favor, pull up as close to Ann's house without being seen. I'm afraid that she and Rick will get themselves hurt. They have their kids."

"Not a problem, Chris. I'm close and will be there in two."

"Thanks Jim." Chris replied

Jumping in the car, Rick and Ann lose no time getting back to Ann's house. When they arrive, Ann jumped out of the car and ran up to the living room window, gun drawn. At the same time, Rick had run around the backside of the house.

Ann could see the silhouette of a human figure moving up the staircase.

Quietly, she entered through the front door.

"There you are." A male voice from the back corner of the dining area said. "We thought you would never get here! Where's your boyfriend?"

Startled, Ann turned toward the sound of the voice, "Who is that?"

"I'm the guy holding one of your kid with a gun to his head." Replied the voice. "One false move, and well, I think you can figure out the rest!" He chuckled.

"Don't hurt my son!" She exclaimed seeing Andrew in front of the man.

"I won't, as long as you give me what I want! Where are the documents and pictures?"

"I don't know what you are talking about." Ann replied

"Oh, I think you do, Ann. Don't make me get rid of this kid like I did your long lost husband!" He chuckled again.

Just then, she saw Rick hiding behind the corner of the living room.

"Wait!" Ann reached her hand out and dropped her weapon. "There. Now you can see I'm not armed. Let him go! Where are my other children?" Ann asks the man.

"Oh, well…I'm afraid that one of 'em didn't fare as well as you might have hoped." The man chuckled again with a laugh that sent chills up Ann's spine.

"Oh my god! You *killed* one of my kids!?" She screamed.

"I think you better pay attention to me, otherwise this one is going to be saying 'bye-bye'! Now, I know that all cops carry an extra piece, Sal! Check her out!" The man says.

"Gladly!"

Ann sees Sal appear from behind the bedroom doorway. With a look of disgust, she lifted her arms for him to frisk her for weapons.

"Ah! Aren't you gonna pull your clothes off for me?" Sal whispered in her ear.

"Sal!" The man shouted "just check her for weapons! For God's sake!"

Sheepishly, Sal resumed checking her for weapons.

"She's clean." He reported and takes a step back from her.

"I'm going to ask one more time, Ann. Where are the documents?"

"Oh god! Please don't hurt him! They're in the bedroom, in my safe, but there's a trick to the combination, you'll have to let me open it!" Ann was shaking, worried about Andrew and wondering if the other boys were alive or not. She was trying not to believe him, but found it difficult not to.

"I'm ok, mom." Andrew told her.

"Shut up!" The man jerked Andrew closer to him.

"Okay! Okay! What do you want me to do?!" Ann screamed at him.

"Sal, Take her into the safe and keep an eye on her!"

Sal followed Ann into the bedroom where she knelt down in front of the safe. Standing behind her, he had the gun pointed at the back of her head "Hurry up, Ann!" He yelled.

She opened the safe, carefully, and reached inside of it to withdraw her husband's hand gun. Holding it close to her, she quickly turned, catching Sal by surprise and shot him in the neck. Gasping for air, he fell to the floor while clutching his throat. Ann quickly jumped up and grabbed Sal's gun. Knowing that the other man had most likely heard the shot, Ann stood perfectly still and waited for a response. Stuffing both guns into her belt, she quickly drug Sal's body into the closet, then headed for the front room.

Hearing the gunfire, the man grabbed Andrew and headed for the vehicle outside with the intention of locking his young hostage in the trunk. Assuming that Sal had just completed the last part of their plan and expecting him to exit the home with the documents, Ramon, shouted toward the house.

"Sal! Get your ass out here with the documents! I got the kid, let's go!"

Hearing Ramon and knowing Sal's condition, Ann headed toward the front of the house.

Rick, having heard Ramon outside, and still not knowing who received the bullet from the shot, headed toward the bedroom as he saw a figure emerge. Hugging himself against the wall, he waited to see who it was.

As the figure approached, Rick realized that it was Ann. With overwhelming relief, Rick let out a heavy sigh.

"Oh, thank God, Ann! Your alive" he whispered, "I thought I might have lost you!"

Startled at the sound of his voice, Ann turned to see Rick in the hallway, "Oh!" Ann exclaimed

"Shh!" Rick whispered as he covered her mouth with his hand. "I need you to be quiet. What happened to Sal?"

Removing his hand from her mouth, Ann pointed toward the bedroom closet and whispered, "He's in there, dead."

"Good! Now, follow me." Rick led the way toward the front room of the house where he heard voices from outside. Peering through the front door window, they discovered Ramon out front standing by the car. Rick turned to Ann,

"Go ahead. He's waiting for someone to come outside. With the porch this dark, he won't be able to tell its you. I will be right behind you!"

Quietly, Ann opened the front door. Giving Rick a hesitant look, she felt his hand gently squeeze her shoulder as she stepped out onto the porch.

At that very moment, Ramon saw a shadow exiting the front door of the house. "Good job, Sal!" He yelled with a laugh.

"Hey thanks!" A female voice replied.

"Huh, wha?" Ramon stammered

"Surprise!" Ann shouted as she pointed Sal's gun at Ramon. "Bye-bye!"

She fired at Ramon who jumped behind the car for safety. Hit in the leg by the bullet, he crawled around to the front of the vehicle and returned fire. Dodging the bullet, Ann jumped back into the house, turning to Rick, she yelled, "You armed?"

"No!" He shouted back. She tossed Sal's gun to Rick as she pulled her own weapon from her waist band.

Slowly, Rick opened the front door again and, both of them crawling on their stomachs, they positioned themselves to get a good visual on Ramon when another shot was fired. Ann heared a muffled cry from beside her when she turned her head and discovered that Rick had received another bullet to his arm. Angry, she fired one round after another, unsure as to whether or not she had hit her target, she stopped to listen and reload.

"Nice try! Not too bad for a female cop!" Ramon yelled from somewhere behind the vehicle.

Just then, police cars appeared in the distance with sirens blaring.

"Hang in there sweetie!" Ann said to Rick, "The cavalry has arrived!"

With Chris' squad car in the lead and four others behind him, they all pulled up to the side of the garage. Immediately, Jack jumped out of the back seat of Chris' car. Ann heard another shot as Jack fell backward to the ground.

"Jack!" Ann screamed

After firing, Ramon crawled around to the other side of the vehicle. Pointing his gun at Chris' car, Ramon began to fire, emptying his magazine. Ann returned fire and shot Ramon in the back of the head and he crumpled to the ground.

As an act of precaution, Ann held her badge over her head and shouted,

"My son is in the trunk of that car! Two other boys are missing."

Cautiously, she began to work her way over to the garage.

Laying on the porch in serious pain, Rick was making an attempt to get up and help Ann. Failing, he fell back down in his own pool of blood.

Chris was slumped over the steering wheel, Ramon had shot him in the chest.

Ann ran to Ramon's vehicle desperately looking for her son. "Andrew!" She shouted, "Andrew? Are you ok?"

Suddenly she heared a thumping noise coming from the trunk of the car. "Andrew!" She shouted "hang on baby! We'll get you out!"

As the officers run to the car to assist in getting Andrew to safety, Rick had somehow managed to crawl over to his friend who is alive, but unconscious. Barely breathing, Rick whispers to Chris,

"Hang in there buddy. Help is on the way."

The fire crew pried open the trunk of the car and found Andrew inside. He was shaken up, but otherwise uninjured.

"Mom!" Andrew shouted as he was assisted out of the vehicle. Laying her hand on Andrews arm to comfort him Ann tells him,

"Lay still, honey. Everything is going to be okay now. Honey, where are your brother and Joey?"

"I think they took them into the garage."

Running toward the garage, Ann has her guard up as she entered.

After securing the area, Ann hollered for the boys.

"Phil! Joe!" She shouted

She heard a faint scuffling noise from somewhere behind another vehicle parked in the back.

Approaching the noise, she headed for the back of the garage.

"Phil! Joe!" She tried again.

"Over here!"

In the far corner of the garage, she found Joey, tied up with bruises all over his face. Phillip was lying, unconscious next to him.

"Oh my God!" Ann exclaimed.

Just then, a shot was fired from behind Ann.

✳✳✳✳✳✳

Ann saw a faint light ahead of her that seemed to be getting closer and closer. Then, out of the light she saw a silhouette of a human form. As it drew closer, a tear formed in each of her eyes as she recognized the form to be Wayne.

"Hi." He said to her

"Hi" replied Ann "Am I dead?"

"Yes, Ann. You are with me now" he told her

"What happened?" she asked him.

"There was a third party involved in all of this. Mike, who used to be a commissioner in Michigan, was still involved and forced to get rid of you before you disclosed any information about the mafia. But when he entered the garage, he saw Laurie pointing a gun at you. He fired two shots, the first one missed her and caught you in the back, the second killed Laurie instantly. I am so sorry, honey. I know that my involvement has cost you not only your life, but Phillip's as well… but the good news is that we are all together in our own Summerville. Just like you used to say, remember? You know Ann, it isn't so bad here. I don't feel any pain. I came back into my body a couple of times, but it's better here." He gave her that smile, the one she loved and knew so well the one that even Wayne could never fake because it stole her heart that very first day.

"They killed Phillip?" she asked him

"Yes, baby. One of them shot him in the chest. Hi didn't feel any pain though. He's up here with me."

From behind him, Ann saw her oldest son

"Hi mom" Phillip said to her "I'm with dad now. I love you."

Tears rolling down her face, Ann couldn't believe what she was seeing. Now she lost both her husband and her oldest son.

"How am I supposed to be okay with this, Wayne? And what about Andrew? He's all alone now."

"Well, honey, no one has found your body yet, the bullet you received hit your spleen. You're life can still be saved without too much difficulty, but if that is what you choose, you will have to get back quickly. Baby, if you want to go back, you still can. But you are going to need to let go of me if that is the decision you have made. We had our time shortened, but you still have a great deal of living to do. I can take care of Phil up here, and you can take care of Andrew down there, if that is what you choose. I never wanted to leave you baby. But I want you to know that I am safe here and will wait an eternity for you. You live your life now and make the decisions you were always so good at making. I can only visit you in your dreams, but Rick will take care of you and you of him. You're doing a great job, honey. You know you stole my heart that day, and now you've got your teeth in it!"

"How am I supposed to go on without you? This hurts too much! You weren't supposed to die that day, remember? We had so many plans ahead of us!"

Ann couldn't help but feel an overwhelming desire to hold on to him as long as she could. She didn't want to see him walk away again.

"It hurts because you think I should be there and I can't because what happened is already passed. Now it's your time to love and be loved by the man that is there with you, I can't go any further until you join me when it's your time. Rick loves you and you him. It's okay, I want you to have a full life, baby. Know that I stole your heart too. You promised to love me for the rest of your life and love me you always will! Moving on with your life is not an act of betrayal. You must continue to live as you would have and always did with me! I love you so much and wait for you, I always will. We built a lifetime together and in doing so, have built an eternity. Follow your heart now, honey. You are making the best decision and I love you for it! I know that you will take good care of all of us. You already committed you're eternal feelings, remember?"

"I love you, Wayne. Don't ever forget that! Check in on us once in a while, okay?" She lost another tear down her cheek.

"You bet baby." He said, "In fact, I will check in on you whenever I can! Mom and dad are here with me as well, and they love you too. We all miss you, and I will see you one day in our Summerville, our own heaven!"

Smiling, Wayne turned from Ann and walked away into the distant light.

Rick, who had entered the room, knelt down next to Ann and gently held her head. As she opened her eyes, Rick whispered to her, "Hey there! I thought we lost you, kiddo! You ok?" he asked

"You know what?" she slowly turned her head toward his, "actually, I think I am, Rick." She gasped and smiled, "Other than the pain I'm in, I think I really am ok!" She slowly closed her eyes and said to him, "I saw Wayne, Rick. He told me that he was okay. I know you don't believe me, but Phillip is dead Rick, go get Joey and Andrew and make sure they're okay. Laurie is dead too."

"Yeah, I know, Mike killed her. He accidently shot you when she jumped out of the way. He feels real bad!" Rick replies with a slight chuckle.

"Good!" Ann said returning the smile the best she could.

Smiling, Rick said, "Don't worry about the rest of us. By the way, how do you know Phillip and Laurie are dead?"

"I just do." Ann said calmly with tears falling down her cheeks.

✳✳✳✳✳✳✳✳✳✳

Ann was never sure if she actually experienced seeing her beloved that day or not. The doctor's never actually confirmed that she had died, but what she did know for certain was that all of those thoughts of taking her own life were gone. She knew that no matter what she did with the rest of her life, Wayne and Philip would be a part of her forever. And that it was ok, because one day, they would all be together again.

Epilogue

Chris and Jack were both critically wounded. They were flown to the nearest trauma center and underwent extensive surgery. Chris who had received a bullet to the heart barely survived. His injuries will prevent him from working for quite some time, but, knowing Chris like Ann did, she expected him to defy the doctors wishes and return to work full time.

Jack was not as lucky. The injuries he received were enough to collapse both lungs. He likely, will never fully recover as the extent of the damage was expected to prevent him from ever having full lung capacity again. Ann thought that now would be a great time to keep him from smoking ever again.

Ann did tell Rick the story of her "out of body experience", which he felt was another way of allowing herself to heal.

Mike is currently under police protection from the Cosa Nostra and Bone Breakers after testifying against Guido and Frankie, although they never showed to the trial. He and Sharon remain married to this day.

Andrew went on as best he could after losing his grandparents, his dad and his only brother. He allowed Rick and Joey into his life and they all promised to work on developing a strong relationship.

Ann had not openly claimed to see or experience her husband's spirit since that day, although she maintains that she can feel him on certain occasions. She supposed that would never leave her, after all, Wayne made a promise to her. She left Phillip's room exactly as he left it and had no intentions of ever changing that. The door to his room remains locked to anyone else. She continued her work with the police department and has been promoted to detective, something she always dreamed of.

Rick and Ann have decided to continue their relationship together. By Ann's request, he has claimed to have left the Bone Breakers life permanently. They plan to marry one day.

Guido and Frankie were never caught. The last report indicated that they had left the country. Ann supposed it was possible they could return one day, although not likely.